2

Story & Art By
Shiro Moriya

Soloist in a Cage

CONTENTS

VOOSH
Chapter 7: The Three Boys
VSH
VSH
VSH
VSH
VSH

HUFF!
HUFF!
VSH
VSH
VSH
VSH
...!
NO MATTER WHERE I TURN... THOSE PRISONERS ARE ON GUARD.
I CAN'T GET NEAR THAT BUILDING...
IF...
IF ONLY THERE WERE SOME PLACE I COULD GET A VIEW OF IT...
I FOUND HER TRACKS!
THIS WAY!
...!

!!
VSH
W-WILL I HAVE TO... FIGHT...?
WHOOSH
SWP

YES, I SEE NOW...
YOU ARE A STRONG ONE...
ZOOON

TAKE IT.
YANK
QUICKLY.
......

HEY LADY, OVER HERE!
A-A CHILD...?
C'MON! HURRY UP!
Slip!
VSH!
drag...
VSH!
MAKE SURE IT'S CLOSED!
VSH!

......
KLONK...
SPLISH
SPLISH

......
SPLISH
SPLISH
SPLISH
SPLISH...
UM...
I MEAN...
TH-THANK YOU FOR SAVING ME...
NO PROB-LEM.

I'M SEBASTIAN.
M-MY NAME IS CHLOE...
CHLOE.
CHLOE.
YEAH.
CHLOE.
UH-HUH...
CHLOE.
I-ISN'T IT DANGEROUS HERE?
THIS DISTRICT IS A TERRIBLE PLACE FOR CHILDREN...
I GUESS...
BUT WE'RE SPECIAL... SO IT'S OKAY.
CHLOE...
......
OH, REALLY?
I SAVED YOU, CHLOE.

I'M THE ONE WHO SAVED YOUR LIFE.
HUH ...?
IN THIS TOWN, IT'S FINDERS KEEPERS.
THE ONE WHO WAS SAVED... BELONGS TO THE PERSON WHO SAVED THEM.
THAT'S WHY...
YOU BELONG TO ME, CHLOE!

SLIDE
HOLD MY HAND.
YES?

WOW.
IT'S JUST LIKE KEITH SAID...
GIRLS REALLY ARE SOFT.
THIS IS THE FIRST TIME I'VE EVER TOUCHED A GIRL.
WE HAVE TO CLIMB THIS.
3B
KLANG
KLANG
KLANG
SCRAPE...

I'M HOME.
LISTEN TO THIS! I FOUND A GIRL!
SWP..!
WELCOME BACK.
YOU'RE LATE TODAY.
......
LOWFAT MILK
WHAT?

WHO ARE YOU...?
HUH...?

I SAVED HER.
CHLOE.
MY CHLOE.
I'M... UM... WELL...
REALLY...
WHERE'D YOU COME FROM?
HEH...
A GIRL.
F-FROM DISTRICT ONE...
WHAT?! ARE YOU KIDDING?!
BY YOUR-SELF?
GRRRRR
I SAVED CHLOE! SHE'S MINE!
KEITH! STOP MAKING PASSES AT CHLOE!

THAT'S WHY CHLOE IS GONNA LIVE HERE WITH US.
!
S-SEBASTIAN.
I-I DON'T THINK I CAN...
YEAH! GREAT IDEA! WHY NOT!
WE NEED A GIRL HERE ANYWAYS...
NO!
WE DON'T KNOW ANYTHING ABOUT HER.
NO NORMAL PERSON COULD MAKE IT ALL THE WAY HERE...
FROM DISTRICT ONE.
ESPECIALLY NOT A GIRL...

WHO CARES ABOUT THAT?
I SAVED CHLOE.
AND I'M GONNA KEEP HER!
YOU DUMMY!
STOP BEING RUDE. SHE'S NOT A DOG!
CLAMOR
CLAMOR
......
E-EXCUSE ME...
D-DO YOU THREE LIVE HERE...?
WELL...
THE ONES LIVING HERE ARE THESE TWO.
I'M THEIR BUDDY, SO I MAKE SURE TO HELP THEM OUT WHENEVER I CAN.
O-OH...
glance
......
I BET THIS MAKES YOU PRETTY CURIOUS.
HUH...?

THAT A NORMAL GROUP OF KIDS LIKE US WOULD LIVE...
IN A DISTRICT WITH THAT PERVERTED GANG ROAMING AROUND.
RIGHT ...?
WELL, THE THING IS...WE'RE NOT YOUR AVERAGE KIDS.
THE ABILITY TO MAKE A LIVING THAT WOULD PUT AN ADULT TO SHAME...
IS WHAT WE'VE BEEN BLESSED WITH.
WE ACTUALLY DO EARN OUR OWN KEEP.
AND NOTHING IS STOLEN, OF COURSE!
OH...! HOW RESOURCEFUL!
HEH... IT'S NOTHING...
LEO, YOU DON'T KNOW ANYTHING! YOU BLOCKHEAD!

YOU CAN AFFORD TO FEED ONE MORE.
I'LL HELP OUT, OF COURSE!
I'M A RESOURCE-FUL KID, AFTER ALL!
LEO DON'T BE SO HARD ON HER.
WAAH! KEITH...!
SAME GOES FOR SEBASTIAN.
SHE COULD BE LIKE A MOTHER FOR YOU GUYS.
PLUS, SHE'S A GIRL.
YOU'VE NEVER EVEN SEEN YOUR MOTHER'S FACE.
WH-WHAT SHOULD I DO...?
THIS WASN'T PART OF THE PLAN...
AND DIDN'T YOU SAY YOU WANTED A BIG FAMILY?
glance
glance
I THINK YOU SHOULD TAKE THIS CHANCE TO GET TO KNOW ONE.
UNTIL THIS VERY MOMENT, YOU'VE NEVER HAD ANY CONTACT WITH A GIRL.

......
NO.
THIS HAS NOTHING TO DO WITH HER BEING A GIRL.
IT'S A HOUSE RULE.
ANY-WAY...
KREEK
NO MATTER HOW LUCKY I MAY BE, I CAN'T ALWAYS RELY ON THAT.
THE ONLY REASON WE'VE SURVIVED THIS LONG...
IS BECAUSE WE'VE AVOIDED GETTING MIXED UP WITH STRANGERS.
WHICH IS WHY WE'RE NOT LETTING A STRANGER IN OUR HOUSE NOW.
SORRY, I KNOW IT'S PRETTY COLD OF US...
BUT IT'S THE TRUTH...

I-IT'S OKAY...I DON'T INTEND TO...
I-I WANT A BIG SISTER.
CHLOE IS GONNA BE MY BIG SISTER.
NO!
FWIP!
GOO...
DON'T CRY...

HUSSH

HUH...?
O-OH... I...I'M SORRY...
PLIP PLIP
HUH...? WH-WHY AM I...?
NOW WHAT'RE WE GONNA DO...? YOUR FATHER ALWAYS SAID TO NEVER MAKE A GIRL CRY!
YOU KNOW THAT A FATHER'S WORD IS ABSOLUTE, RIGHT?
JUST...
JUST FOR A LITTLE WHILE...
IN...IN EXCHANGE...
?
Yay!
?

WE'RE GOING TO PUT YOU TO WORK.
I WON'T LET YOU DOWN!
NOT YOU!

I HAVE A GOOD VIEW...
OF THAT BUILDING FROM HERE...
THIS MAY BE A GOOD OPPORTUNITY... AFTER ALL...

Mo	Tu	We	Th	Fr	Sa	Su

Memo No.____________

Date / /

Mo Tu We Th Fr Sa Su

Memo No.

Date / /

Mo	Tu	We	Th	Fr	Sa	Su

Memo No.____________

Date / /

Mo	Tu	We	Th	Fr	Sa	Su

Memo No.____________

Date / /

Chapter 8:
A Mysterious Place
chirp
chirp
SEBASTIAN! KEITH IS HERE TO PICK YOU UP.

SHEESH... LOOK AT THIS. A BUTTON IS LOOSE.
OH.
G-GOOD MORN-ING...
MORNIN'. YOU SLEEP WELL?
YEAH... I APPRE-CIATE IT...
GLAD TO HEAR THAT...
HMM...
STARE!
.....?

I'M JEALOUS OF THESE GUYS.
LIVING WITH A PERSON LIKE YOU...WHO WOULDN'T FALL IN LOVE?!
UH... W-WELL...
TH-THAT'S NOT...
KEITH!
STOP FLIRTING WITH CHLOE!
YIP! YIP!
CHLOE IS MINE!
DUMMY, SHE DOESN'T BELONG TO ANYONE.
STOP QUARRELING AND GET TO WORK.
SEE YOU LATER, CHLOE.
BE A GOOD GIRL.
UM... O-OKAY. HAVE A NICE DAY.

SLAM
UM... THAT IS... THANK YOU FOR THE CLOTHES.
HMM...? OH, SURE.
KEITH... WHAT A PAIN. I GUESS HE'S WHAT YOU'D CALL A PROMISCUOUS KID.
HUH? OH...I SUPPOSE SO...
PROMISSKYU ...?
CLEANING, LAUNDRY, COOKING...
THEY'RE JUST MY FATHER'S HAND-ME-DOWNS ANYWAYS.
BESIDES... THOSE CLOTHES AREN'T EXACTLY COMPENSATION.
THERE'S A LOT I'LL BE ASKING YOU TO DO FROM NOW ON.
HOW-EVER...
WHAT I NEED THE MOST IS...

COME WITH ME.
KNOCK
KNOCK
I'M COMING IN.
CLICK
......
KA-CHIK

I'D LIKE YOUR HELP IN TAKING CARE OF MY FATHER...
BEEP
BEEP
BEEP
BEEP
......

I KNOW. IT'S REPULSIVE SEEING HIM LIKE THIS...
N-NO... OF COURSE NOT...
THREE YEARS AGO, MY FATHER SUDDENLY BECAME ILL...
NOW HE CAN BARELY MOVE.
I UNDER-STAND...IF YOU CAN'T DO IT.
FROM A STRANGER'S POINT OF VIEW, IT MUST BE DISGUST-ING...
NO, I DON'T MIND.
I'M SORRY... I DIDN'T MEAN TO SEEM REPULSED.
I JUST DIDN'T KNOW, SO I WAS A LITTLE STARTLED...
I'LL HELP YOU... LOOK AFTER HIM.
....
THANK YOU. YOU CAN START TOMOR-ROW...

INK
-BLACK
INK
-BLACK

......
WHOOSH...
THAT MYSTERIOUS BUILDING...

THAT MEANS THAT LOCKE...
I DON'T UNDER-STAND IT, BUT THERE ARE CHILDREN ALIVE HERE...
IN A DISTRICT WITH A MURDEROUS GANG ROAMING AROUND...
ARE CHILDREN, LIVING THEIR LIVES NORMALLY....
SURELY MUST BE TOO...
I SEE.
VERY INTER-ESTING...
SO, YOU'RE SEARCHING FOR YOUR YOUNGER BROTHER.
HMPH...

I HOPE HE'S STILL ALIVE.
JUMP!

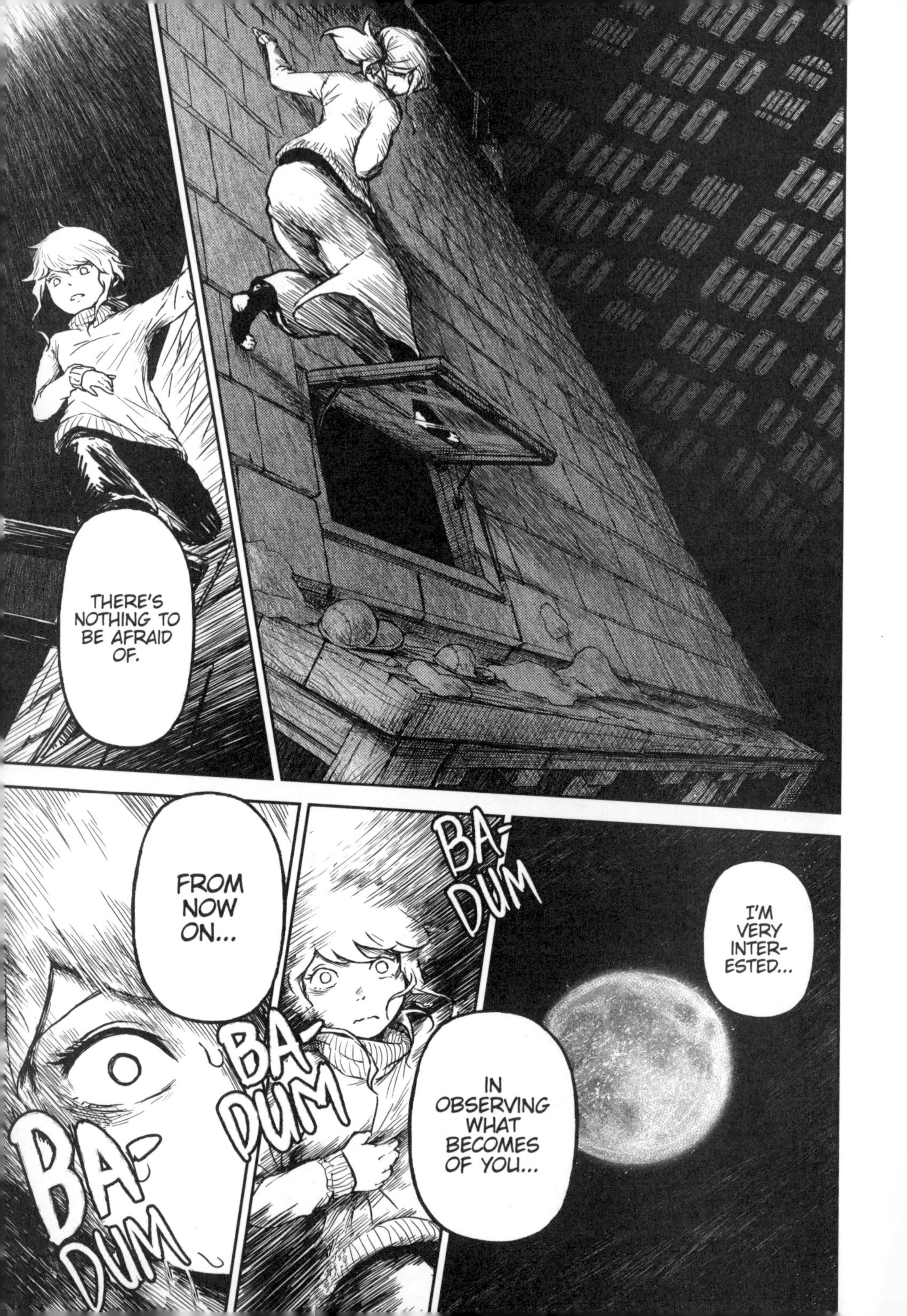
THERE'S NOTHING TO BE AFRAID OF.
I'M VERY INTER-ESTED...
IN OBSERVING WHAT BECOMES OF YOU...
BA-DUM
FROM NOW ON...
BA-DUM
BA-DUM

SPLASH
......

Uh... Ugh...
UGH...
UUNGH...

KNOCK KNOCK
HE SEEMS TO BE CRYING OUT IN PAIN...
Ugh...
Uugh...
UH... EXCUSE ME...
A- ARE YOU OKAY...?
KA-CHIK
......
BEEP
BEEP
!

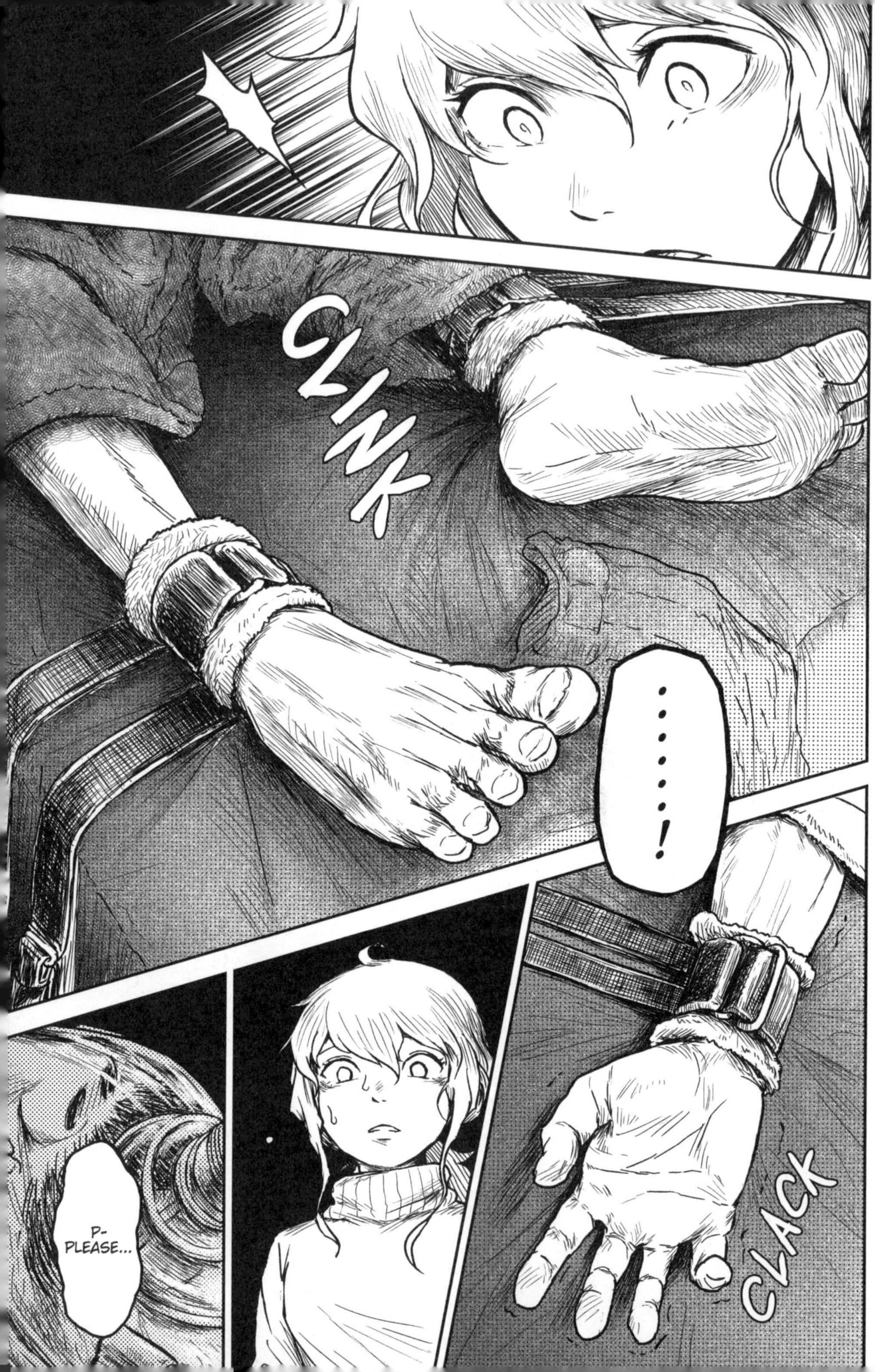
CLINK
......!
CLACK
P-
PLEASE...

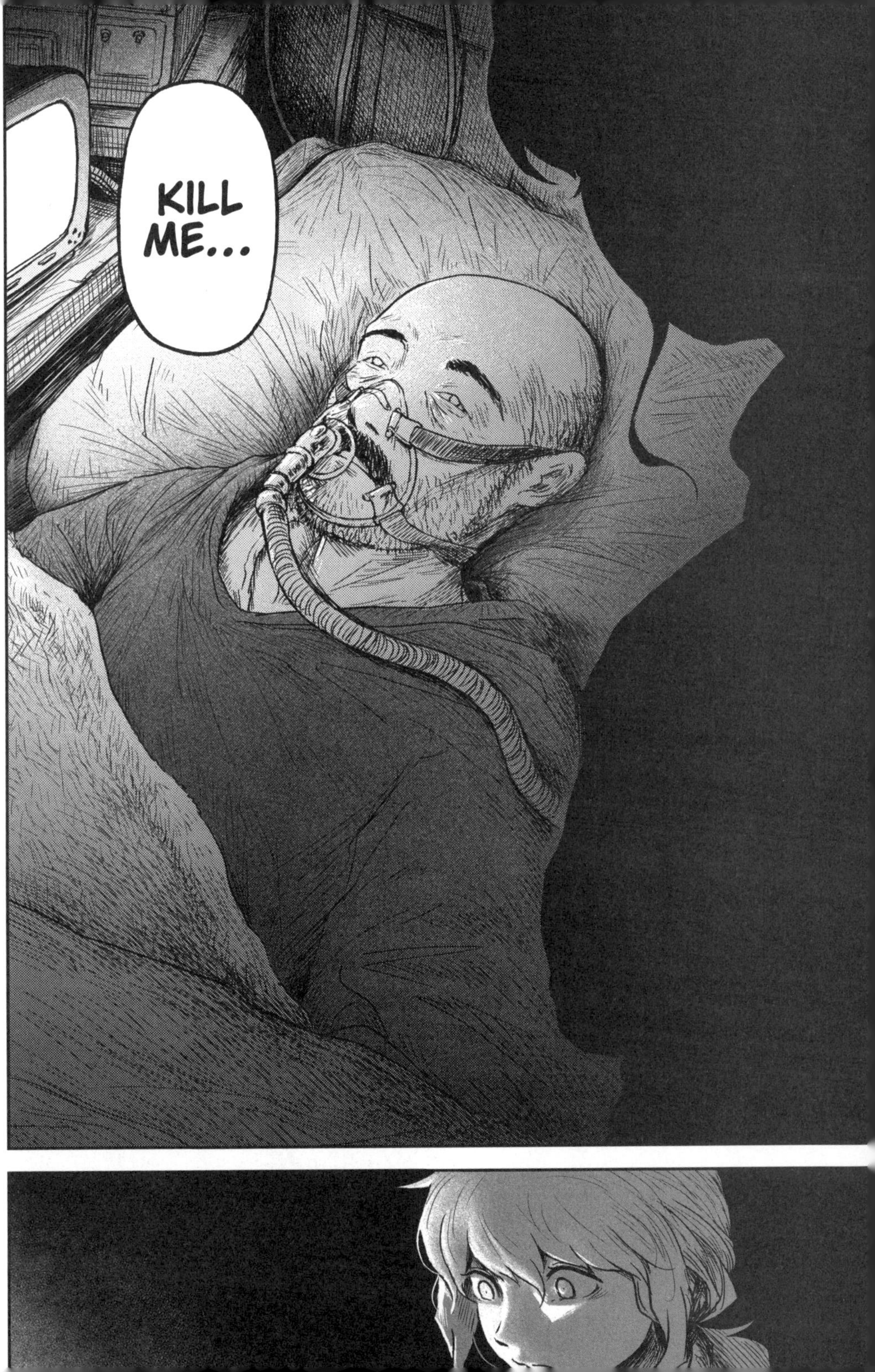
KILL ME...

KLINK
Chapter 9: The Delta Inquisitor
SAFE MODE STARTUP...
KLAK KLAK KLAK
SUPPORT REQUEST COR-RESPON-DENCE INTER-RUPTED.
VMM VMM
COMMU-NICATION EQUIPMENT DAMAGED.
COL-LABORA-TION WITH SECURITY OFFICERS NOT POSSIBLE.
VMM
POWER RE-COVERY RATE 62%
SHIFTING TO FULLY AUTOMATED SYSTEM.

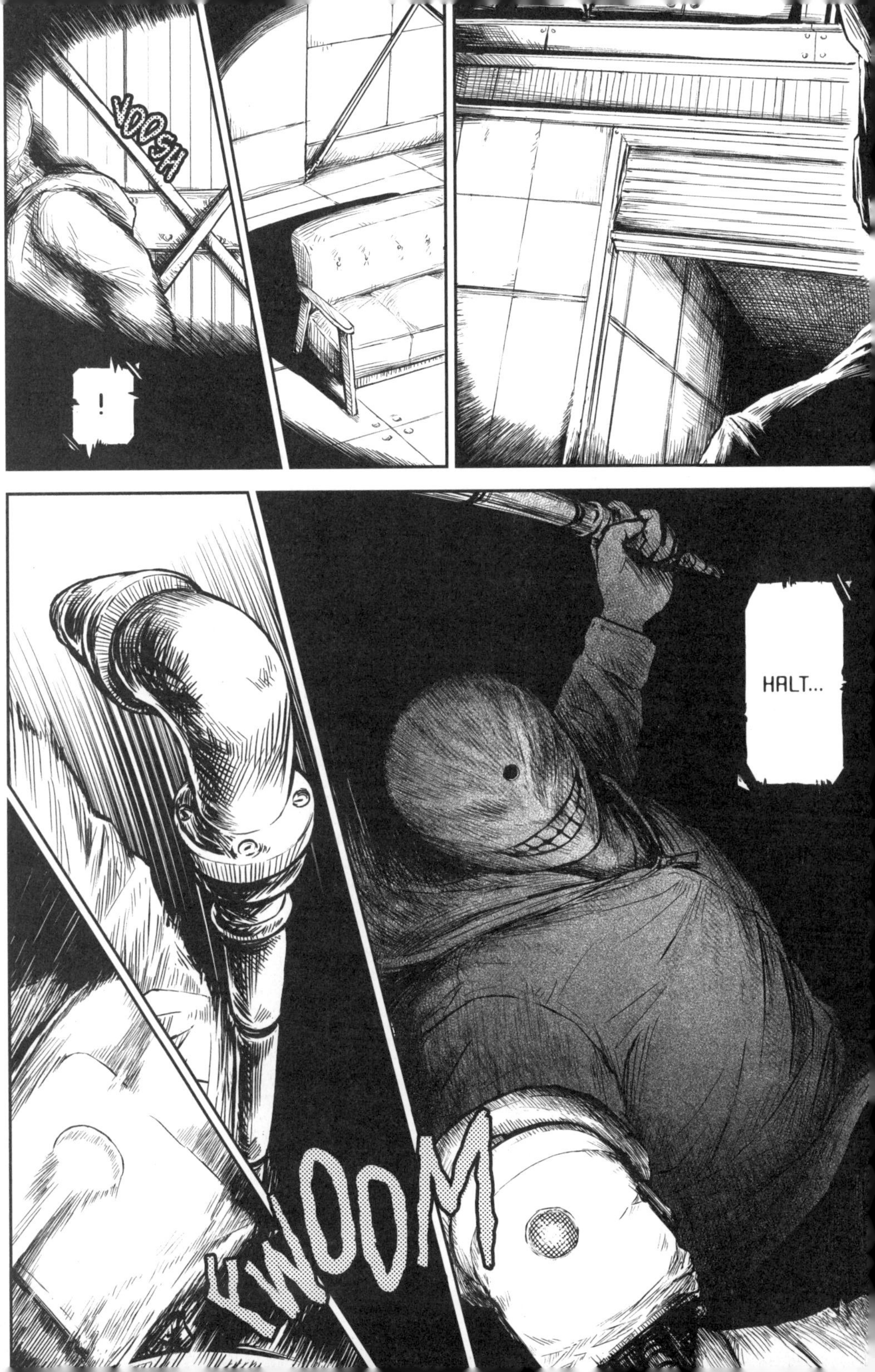
VOOSH
!
HALT...
WOOM

SLASH

LEVEL 4 ALERT.
ATTACKERS TO BE IM-MEDIATELY ELIMINATED.
KER-KLAK
WEEEN
VSHH
WARNING!
RUSH

LEVEL 5 ALERT.
ZWSH
SHIIII I I INGO

ZOON ZOON
MAXIMUM LEVEL ALERT.
ELIMINATE ALL IN IMMEDIATE VICINITY.
WARNING!

HM...
GAAHAHH!
KLINK
KLINK
FWOOM
WHRR
POP

!
ROOOOAR
WEEN
KLIK
KLUNK
KEE
KEE

SNAP
FWOOOSH

WHAM
CRACK

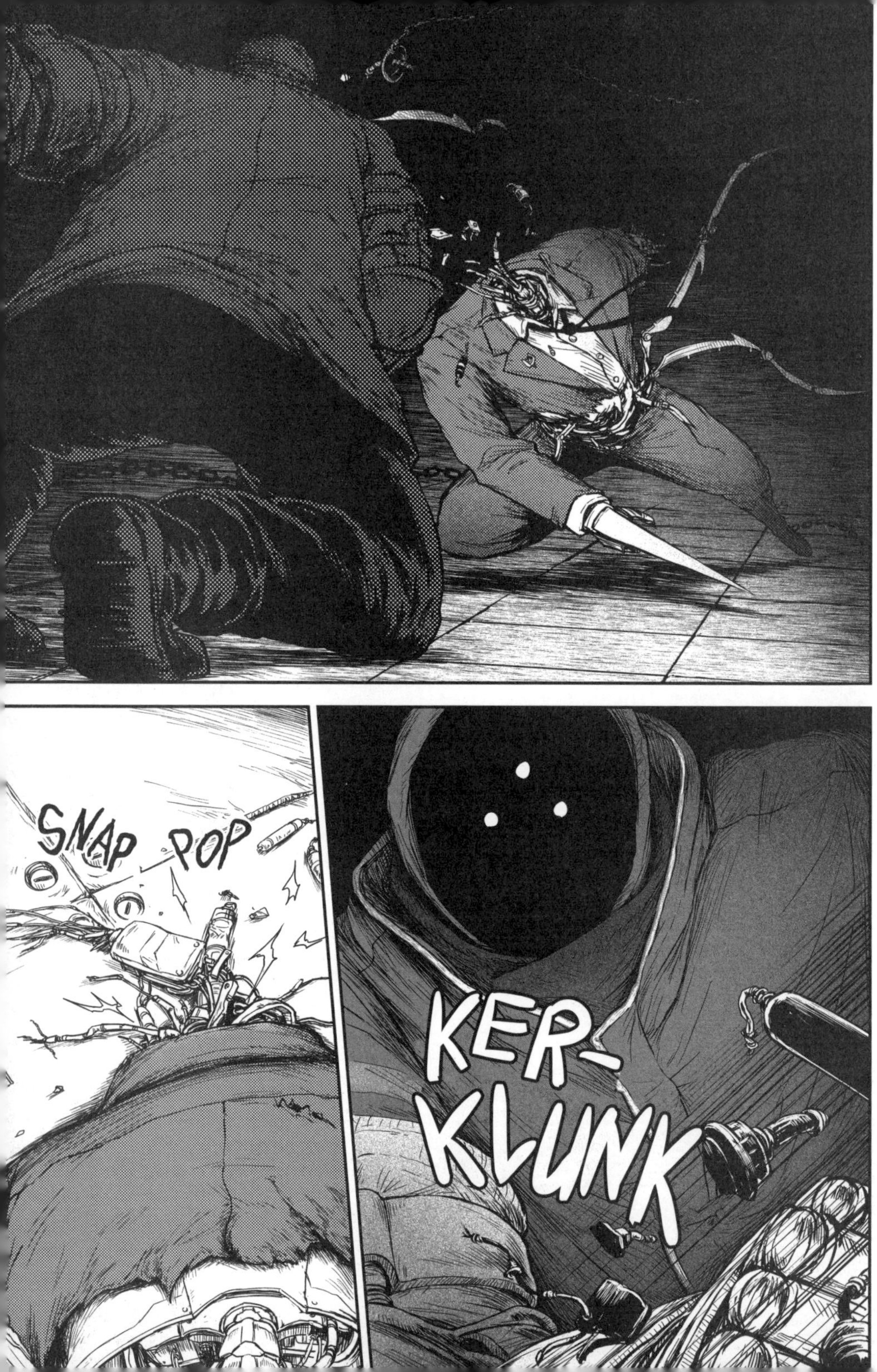
SNAP
POP
KER-
KLUNK

KLOINK
...!
CLAP
CLAP
CLAP
Whoa!
Seriously...
I KNEW YOU COULD DO IT!
BRINGING DOWN A MONSTER LIKE THAT IN ONE BLOW WHEN EVEN A LARGE GROUP OF MEN DIDN'T HAVE A CHANCE.
YOU'RE INVINCIBLE!
THIS GAME BORES ME...
ONE-ON-ONE, IT'S LIKE FIGHTING AN ANT.
THE TROUBLE-SOME PART...
IS THAT WE'RE DEALING WITH AN ARMY OF ANTS.

AN ARMY OF ANTS...
BASICALLY, WE HAVE NO HOPE OF WINNING IN A MASS FIGHT...
KOBA-YASHI.
YES?
HOW MANY YEARS... HAVE WE BEEN PLAY-ING THIS GAME?
POOF
OVER TEN YEARS.
THUD
I'M TIRED OF THIS BULLSHIT...
SIGH...
HOW LONG'S HE GONNA MAKE US WAIT...
THAT OLD MAN, YOSHIKI.

KEITH. ARE THE CHILDREN... AT THE FACTORY...
ALL DOING WELL...?
YEAH...
WE'RE MANAGING PRETTY GOOD.
THERE'S A KID FROM ANOTHER DISTRICT THAT CAME TO MY FACTORY!
HE WAVES TO ME SOMETIMES!
I SEE.
LEO... HOW ARE THINGS IN DESIGN?
GOING SMOOTHLY, FOR THE MOST PART.
WE'RE FOCUSING ON DESIGNING THE POWER UNIT NOW.
WE'LL NEARLY BE DONE AS SOON AS THE ENGINE TEST IS FINISHED.
I SEE.

BY THE WAY...
I'VE NOTICED THAT A GIRL HAS BEEN LOOKING AFTER ME RECENTLY...
YEAH! THAT'S CHLOE!
MY CHLOE!
I'M GRATEFUL. BUT LEO...
YOU'RE STILL IGNORING MY DECISIONS, AS ALWAYS...
N-NO, I'M NOT... IT'S JUST THAT... KEITH AND SEBASTIAN...
IT'S OKAY... PLEASE CONVEY MY GRATITUDE....
FLYING MOLE
......

I KNEW IT...
AFTER ALL, THEY SEEM SO HAPPY...
I MUST HAVE MISHEARD HIM.
"KILL ME..."
I'M FEELING QUITE WELL TODAY...
WON'T YOU... LOOSEN THESE HANDCUFFS A BIT...?
...!
FLYING MOLE

BEEP
BEEP
FATHER...
I'M SORRY, BUT...
I CAN'T DO THAT...
SORRY...
I SEE...

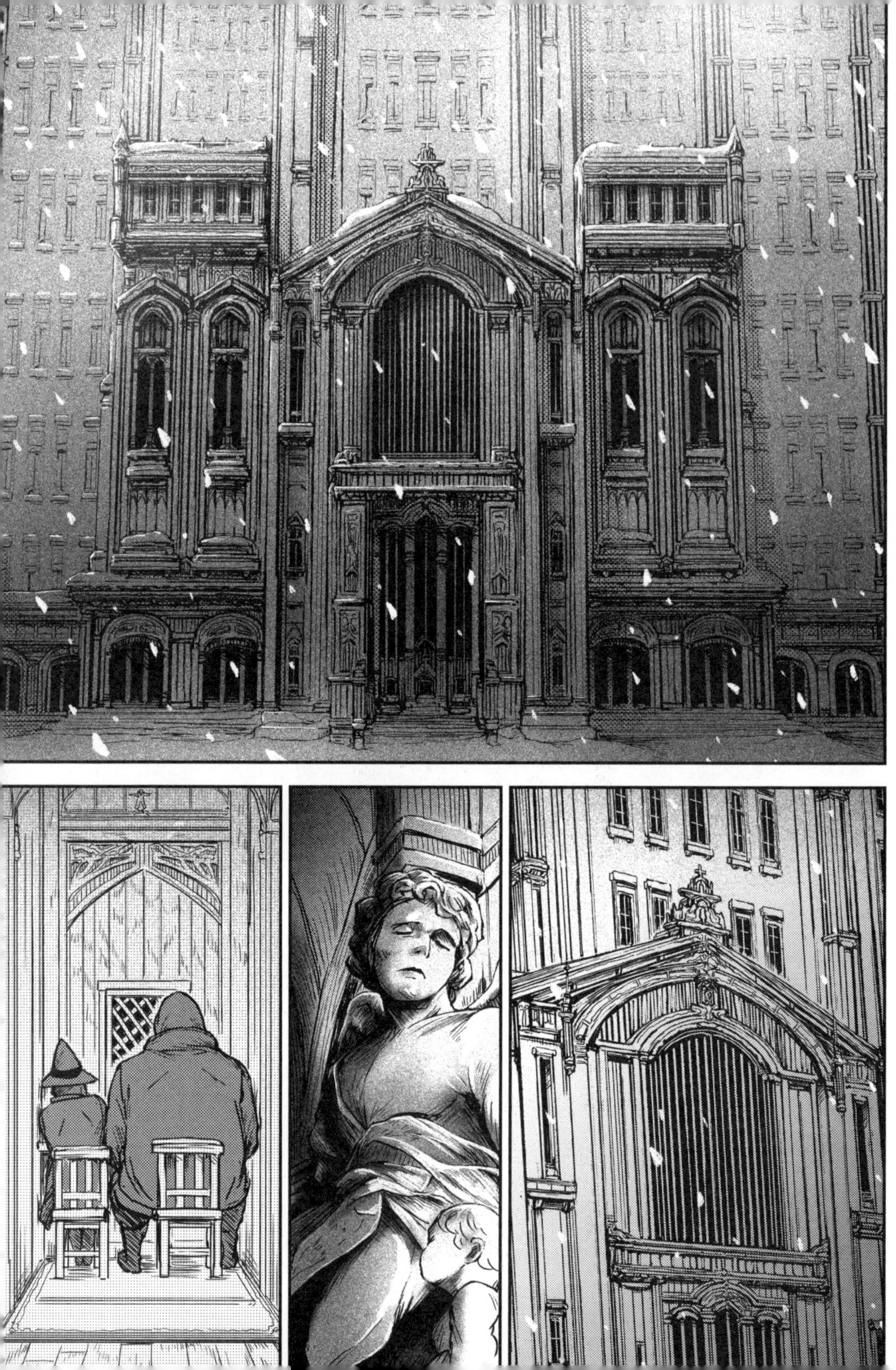

WELCOME, DELTA IN-QUISITOR, KOBAYASHI...
NOW, JOIN HANDS AND CONFESS...
I WAS BORN AND RAISED IN THIS CITY, AND NOW I'VE BEEN HERE OVER TWENTY YEARS.
HAVE I BEEN CLEANSED OF MY SINS?
MY TIME MUST HAVE ARRIVED.
BE PATIENT AND FOLLOW THE WILL OF GOD.
IF YOU PUT YOUR FAITH IN GOD, HE WILL ANSWER YOU.
I'VE BELIEVED AND TRIED MY HARDEST ALL THESE YEARS, HAVEN'T I?
C'MON, THOSE BRATS OBEY EVERY WORD I SAY.
AIN'T THAT A GOOD DEED?
WOULD IT BE SO BAD TO RECEIVE THE GRACE OF GOD, EVEN A LITTLE?

IMPATIENCE WILL EVENTUALLY DISTORT ANY REVELATION INTO AN INTER-PRETATION FOR YOUR OWN SELF-INTEREST.
SOME DAYS AGO, A MOB GATHERED BY THE FENCE IN DISTRICT ONE.
AMONG THEM WERE THOSE WHO BELIEVE THAT THE FRESH BLOOD OF CHILDREN IS GOD'S GIFT.
YOU MUST NOT BECOME LIKE THEM.
CLATTER
DON'T CONFUSE ME WITH THOSE PERVERTS!
THEN HAVE FAITH.

GOD'S MESSAGE HAS NOT CHANGED.
NOAH IS NEAR.
ONLY TRUE BELIEVERS WILL SENSE THIS.
EVEN SO, IT'S BEEN TEN YEARS ALREADY...
HAVE FAITH.

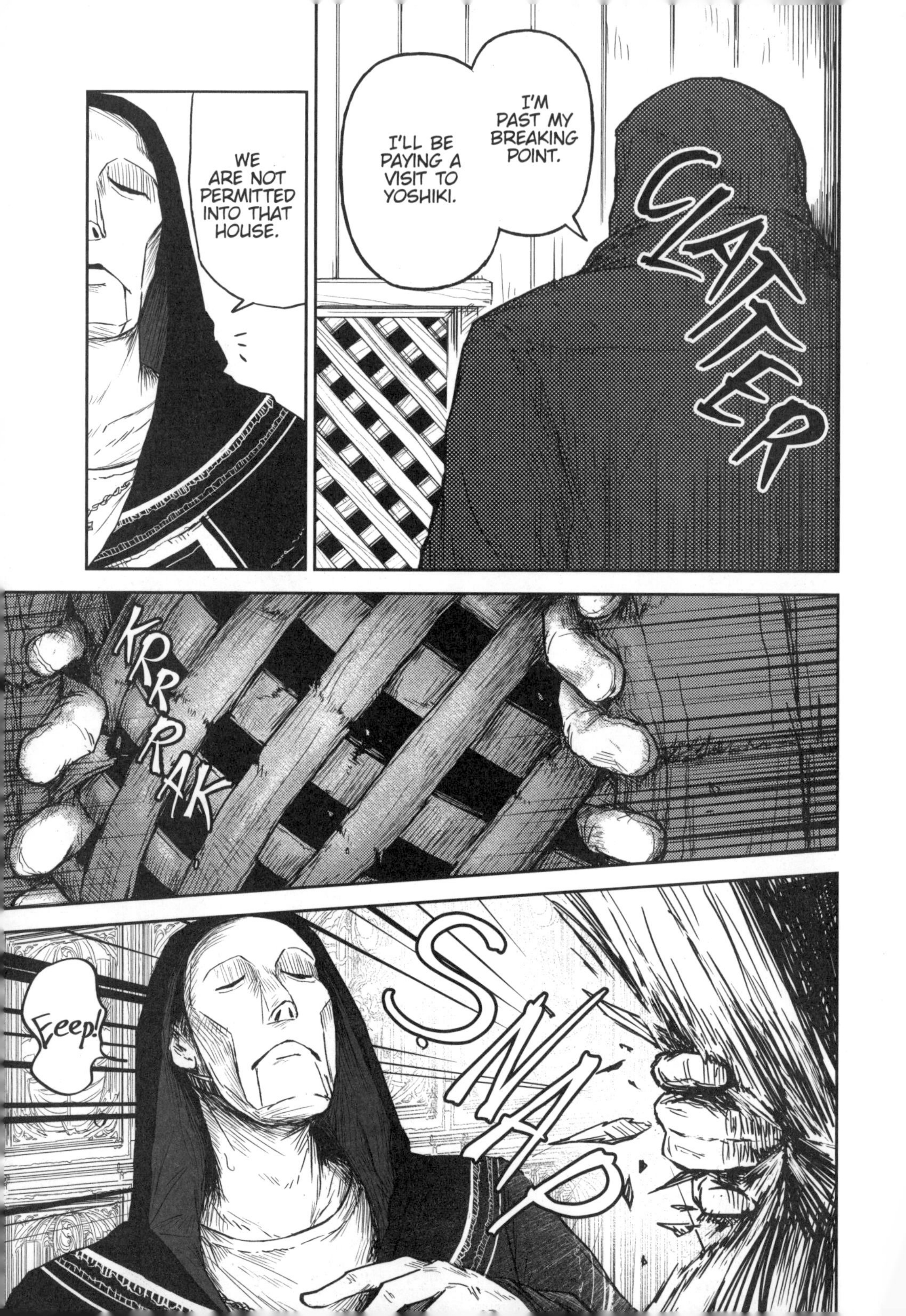
I'M PAST MY BREAKING POINT.
I'LL BE PAYING A VISIT TO YOSHIKI.
CLATTER
WE ARE NOT PERMITTED INTO THAT HOUSE.
KRRRAK
SNAP
Eeep!

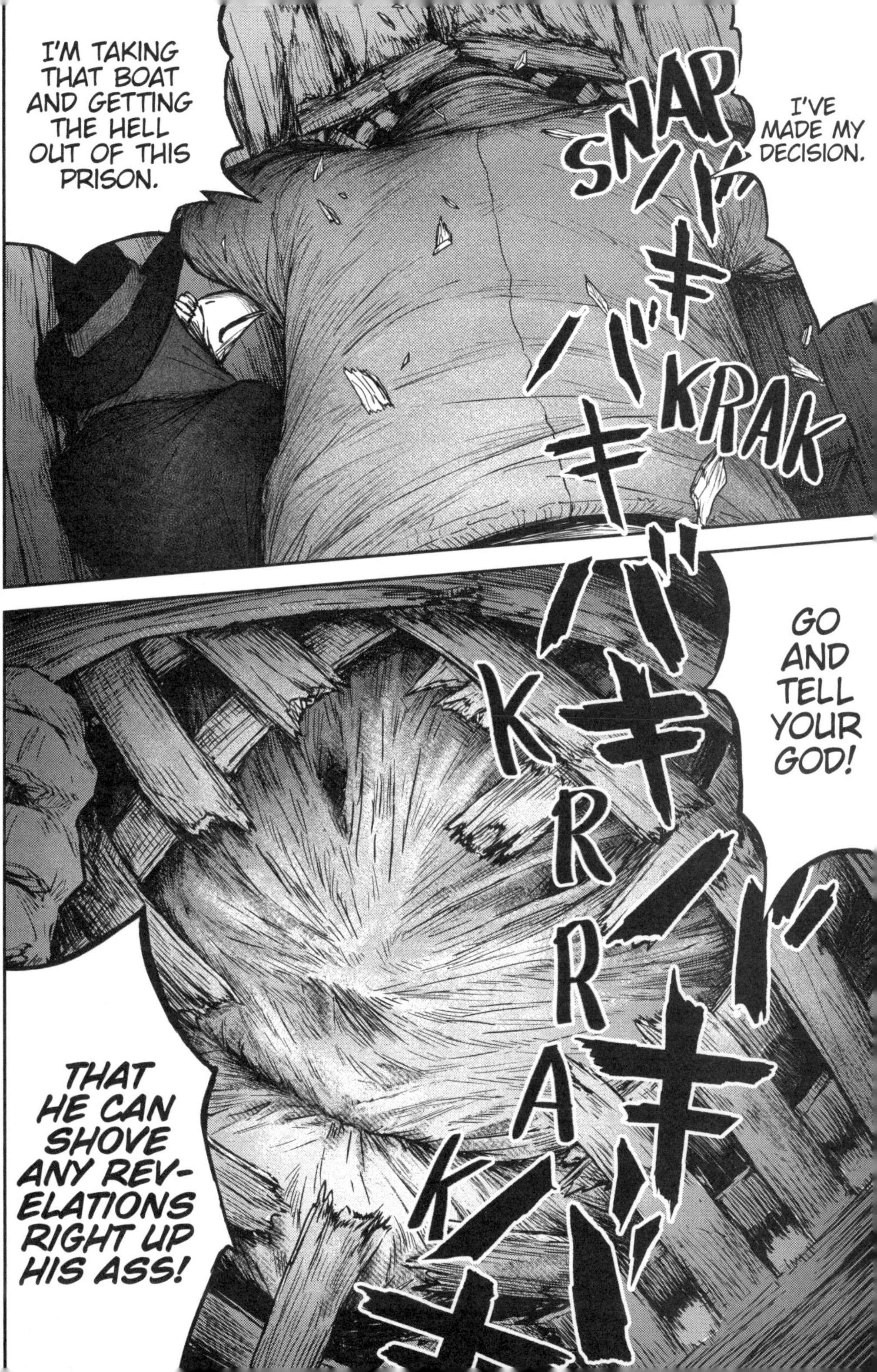
I'VE MADE MY DECISION.
I'M TAKING THAT BOAT AND GETTING THE HELL OUT OF THIS PRISON.
SNAP
KRAK
GO AND TELL YOUR GOD!
KRRAK
THAT HE CAN SHOVE ANY REV-ELATIONS RIGHT UP HIS ASS!

Chapter 10: The Propped-Up Heart

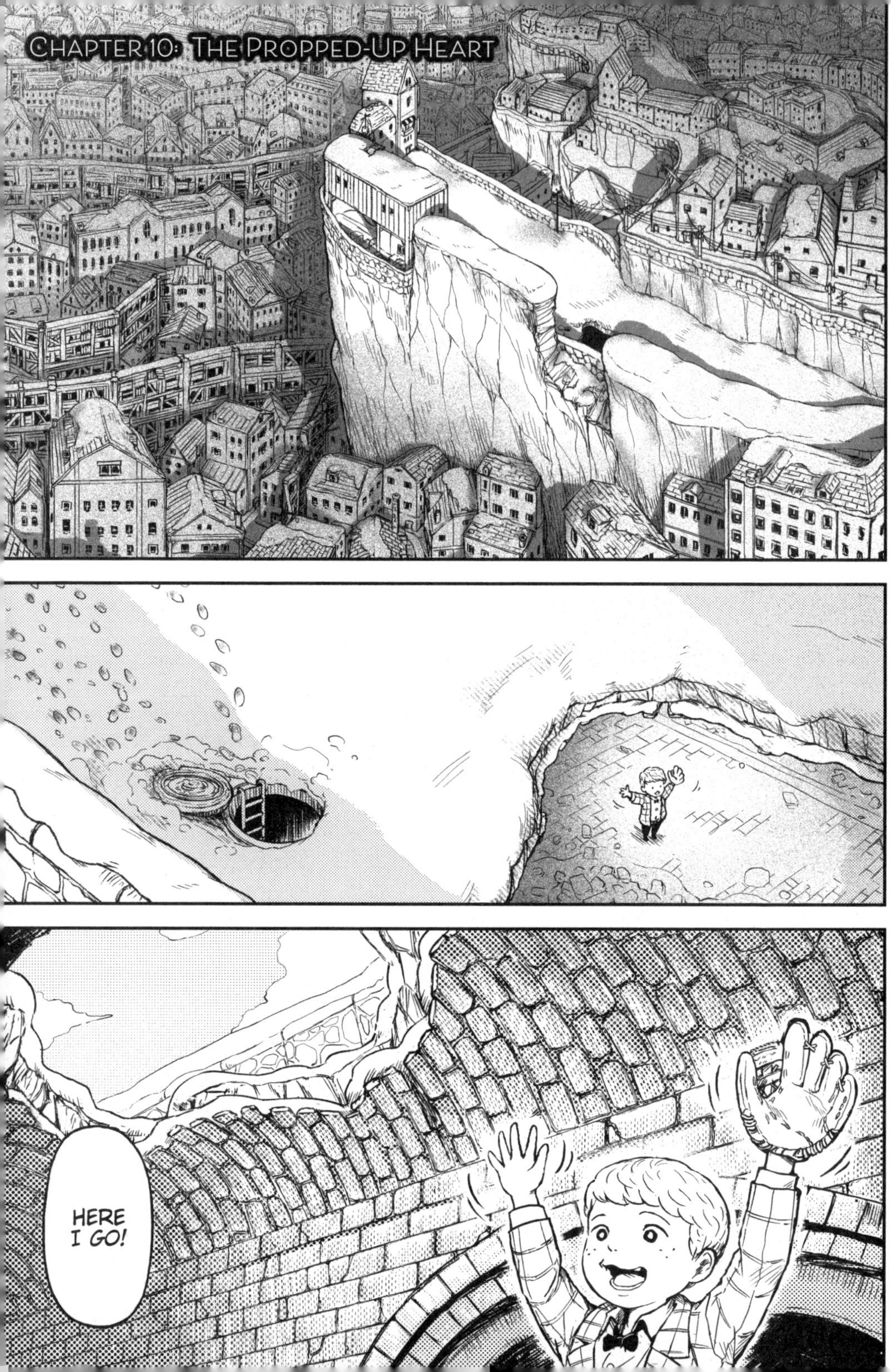

FWOOM
AT LEAST TRY TO CATCH IT...
WHOOSH
HA!
東洋医学
Oriental Medicine
WESTERN MEDICINE
FWIP

......
IS...IS THAT FOR YOUR FATHER...?
YEAH...
I'M NOT A DOCTOR, SO I DON'T UNDERSTAND MOST OF THIS...
BUT I WANT TO LEARN AS MUCH ABOUT HIS DISEASE AS POSSIBLE.
I SEE...
UM...
A-ACTU-ALLY...
I HEARD YOUR FATHER GROANING RECENTLY...
I-IT'S POS-SIBLE...
THOSE SHACKLES... MAY BE TOO TIGHT...
......

BECAUSE OF FATHER'S TOSSING AND TURNING...
HIS RESPIRATOR AND IV DRIP HAVE COME LOOSE MORE THAN ONCE.
THAT'S WHY I HAVE NO CHOICE BUT TO TIE HIM DOWN.
OH...
I KNOW IT LOOKS BAD...
BUT HIS LIFE DEPENDS ON IT...SO TRY NOT TO TAKE THEM OFF, OKAY?
O-OF COURSE...
Uh-oh.
boink
CHLOE! GET MY BALL!

toss
......
A BABY.
OH, YEAH... THAT'S MY LITTLE BROTHER, LOCKE.
THAT IS... WE GOT SEPARATED...
AND I'M SEARCHING FOR HIM.
ARE YOU SAYING...YOU CAME ALL THIS WAY TO SEARCH FOR YOUR BROTHER...?
Y-YEAH...
...!

NOW I UNDERSTAND...
......
COULD I BORROW ONE OF THESE PHOTOS?
HUH?
......
...!
HE MAY HAVE AN IDEA WHO YOUR BROTHER IS.
KEITH IS IN CHARGE OF ALL THE KIDS IN THE CITY WHO WORK IN THE FACTORY.

THAT SAID, YOU SHOULDN'T GET YOUR HOPES UP.
OH... UM... WELL...
THANKS ANYWAY.
I'M SORRY I TRIED TO KICK YOU OUT...
WHEN YOU... FIRST CAME HERE...
I NEVER IMAGINED YOU WERE SO DEDICATED TO YOUR FAMILY.
IT MAY BE RUDE TO SAY THIS TO A PERSON IN YOUR POSITION, BUT...
I FEEL AT EASE NOW, AFTER GETTING TO KNOW YOU.
THAT PRECIOUS PERSON YOU WANT TO PRO-TECT...

THE ONE WHO IS BY YOUR SIDE...
AND IS ALWAYS THERE FOR YOU.

THAT ALONE IS ENOUGH TO PUT ONE'S HEART AT EASE.
I UNDER-STAND HOW YOU FEEL...
ABOUT THAT PRECIOUS PERSON OF YOURS.
I HOPE... YOU CAN FIND YOUR BROTHER.
ME TOO.

THIS IS GRAVE INDEED...
IT HAS BECOME JUST AS WE'D FEARED.
THE BRAIN-WASHING OF THE INQUISITORS IS NO LONGER EFFECTIVE.
IT HAS BECOME DIFFICULT TO SUPPRESS THEM, LET ALONE PASS ALONG OUR ANNUNCIATIONS.

WE'VE KEPT THEM WAITING TOO LONG... THEY'RE AT THE POINT OF VIOLENCE.
WE MUST MAKE A MOVE...!
THEIR VIOLENCE IS ALSO WITHIN THE SCOPE OF MY INTENTIONS.
YES, BUT... THAT MUSCLE-BOUND MONSTER FROM DELTA IS HEADED TOWARD SERGEANT YOSHIKI.
IF THERE'S EVEN THE SLIGHTEST POSSIBILITY OF PUTTING THE SERGEANT IN DANGER, IT COULD AFFECT THE COMPLETION OF THE ARK.
IF WE'RE CARELESS, ALL OF OUR PLANS COULD BE FOR NAUGHT...
IS THERE NOTHING YOU CAN DO, FATHER?
THERE'S NO NEED TO PANIC.
EVEN WITH THE DELTA INQUISITOR. ON THE MOVE, SERGEANT YOSHIKI'S SITUATION HAS NOT CHANGED.
YES...B-BUT...
TH-THAT IS...IF SOMETHING WERE TO HAPPEN TO SERGEANT YOSHIKI, THE ARK...
TCH!
Tch?

RRRRGH...
BE SILENT!
I HAVEN'T FAILED YOU YET...
AND YOU STILL CAN'T TRUST ME?
O-OF COURSE WE TRUST YOU! Y-YOU ARE THE MOST MAGNIFICENT TRICKSTER!
THEN STOP LOSING YOUR HEADS AND GO GET THOSE MORONS UNDER CONTROL!
I AM GOD. DO YOU UNDER-STAND?

IF YOU OBEY ME...
YOU WILL HAVE PASSAGE ON THE ARK.
I'LL SET THE LOT OF YOU PATHETIC LIVESTOCK FREE OF THIS PRISON...
SO QUIT SQUEALING IN FEAR.
AND CONTINUE WORSHIPPING ME AS YOU ALWAYS HAVE.
RATTLE RATTLE

SQUOOOSH
SPLISH
THANK YOU...
FOR EVERY-THING.
......
DON'T WORRY... I'M HAPPY...TO TALK WITH YOU.
OH, I'M SORRY...
I-I WOKE YOU UP.

IT MAY HAVE BEEN A COINCIDENCE... BUT WE'RE LUCKY YOU ENDED UP IN OUR HOME.
I'VE BEEN HEARING ABOUT YOU FROM MY SONS...
YOU'VE DONE A LOT FOR THEM.
NO, THEY'RE THE ONES WHO SAVED *ME*...
THEY TOOK ME IN EVEN THOUGH I WAS A COMPLETE STRANGER...
NOT ONLY THAT...
THE FACT THAT CHILDREN ARE LIVING IN THIS DISTRICT...
HAS TRULY SET ME AT EASE.
I-I WAS SO HAPPY KNOWING THAT...
IN THIS CITY...
IN THIS DISTRICT... I'VE TAUGHT CHILDREN TO SURVIVE, FROM THE TIME THEY WERE BABIES.
IN ORDER TO PROTECT THEM...
I'VE SPREAD MY KNOWLEDGE, TEACHING EVERY ONE OF THEM.

WHAT THOSE CHILDREN DESIRE...
CANNOT BE MEDDLED WITH.
AS LONG AS THEY HAVE THE KNOWLEDGE TO ACHIEVE IT...
THAT'S WHY...THIS DISTRICT HAS BECOME A HAVEN WHERE CHILDREN THRIVE.
AND YET, AT THE SAME TIME...THEY HAVE NO ESCAPE...
...?
I'M SORRY.
THIS MAY BE A BIT CONFUSING FOR YOU...
TH- THAT'S OKAY.
......
I HAVEN'T TALKED TO ANYONE LIKE THIS IN SO LONG...
I'M FEELING QUITE WELL TODAY...

I CAN WIPE MYSELF DOWN...
WON'T YOU PLEASE...
TAKE THESE SHACKLES OFF OF ME FOR A SHORT WHILE?
......
OH...
....
DON'T MIND LEO'S INSTRUCTIONS.
HE TENDS TO BE A TAD PARANOID...
HE'S SIMPLY OVERWORRIED ABOUT MY CONDITION.
THOSE CHILDREN TAKE GOOD CARE OF ME...
BUT THE LEAST I CAN DO IS LOOK AFTER MYSELF WHEN I WAKE UP.
NOT ONLY THAT, BUT I FEEL BAD MAKING YOU DO THIS...
I-I DON'T MIND AT ALL...
WELL...

I KNOW THAT THEIR EXCESSIVE CARE COMES FROM A PLACE OF LOVE.
IT TRULY WARMS MY HEART.
JUST MY LEFT HAND IS ENOUGH.
SLIP
KLINK KLINK
OF COURSE ...
THANK YOU...

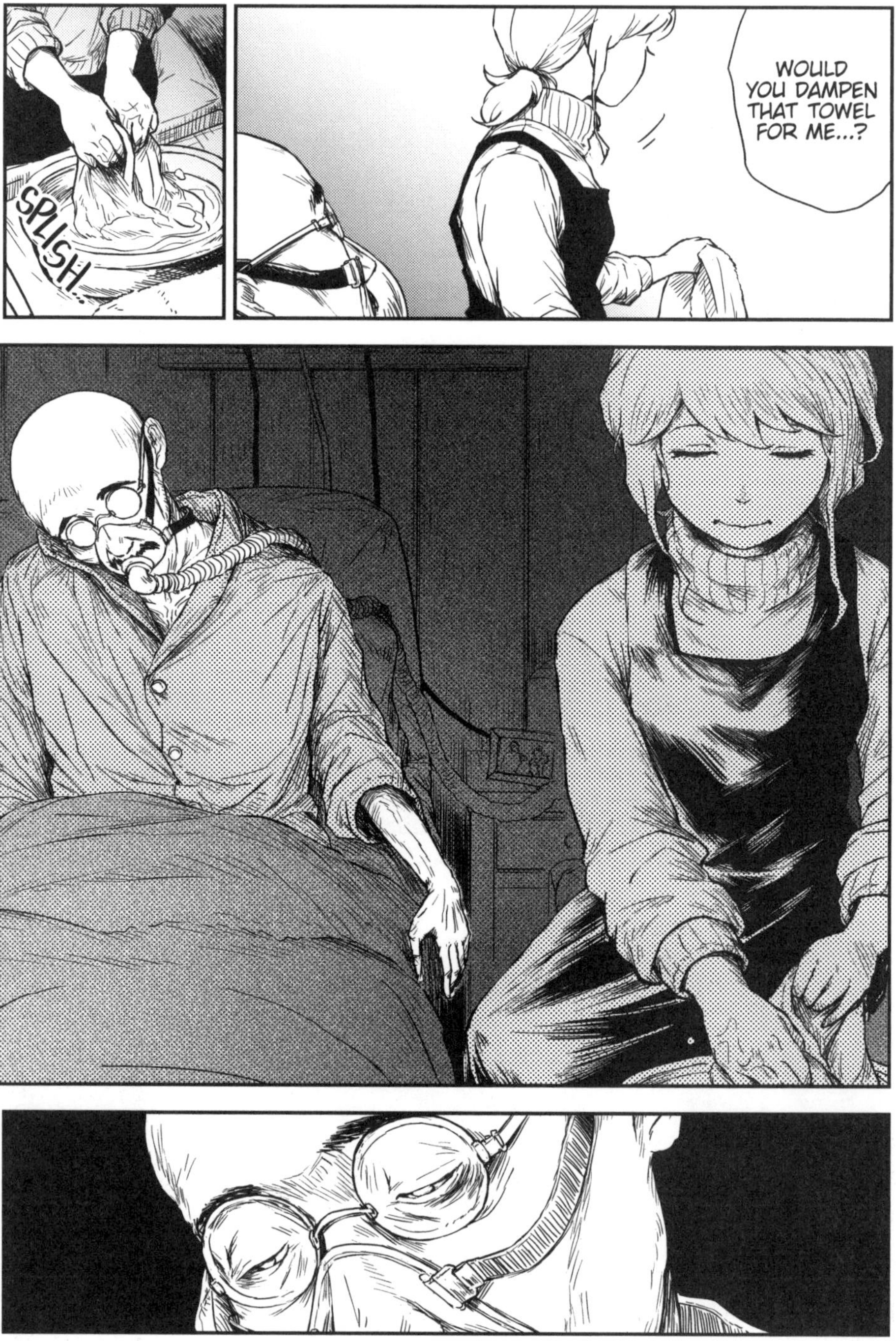
SPLISH...
WOULD YOU DAMPEN THAT TOWEL FOR ME...?

......
LEO, IN PARTICULAR, IS SUCH A KIND CHILD...
SLIDE
I WAS SO HAPPY BEING A FATHER TO THOSE BOYS...

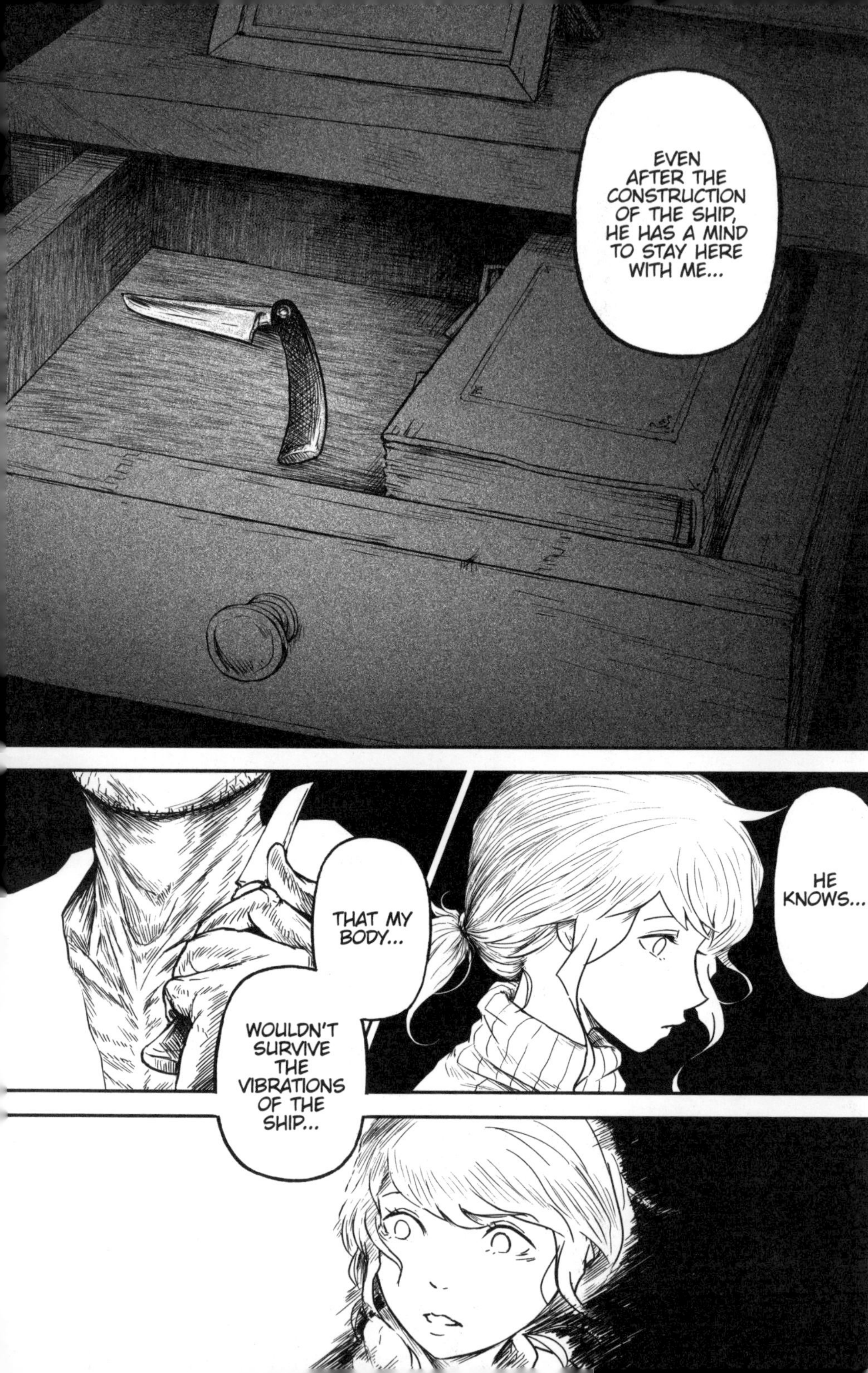
EVEN AFTER THE CONSTRUCTION OF THE SHIP, HE HAS A MIND TO STAY HERE WITH ME...
HE KNOWS...
THAT MY BODY...
WOULDN'T SURVIVE THE VIBRATIONS OF THE SHIP...

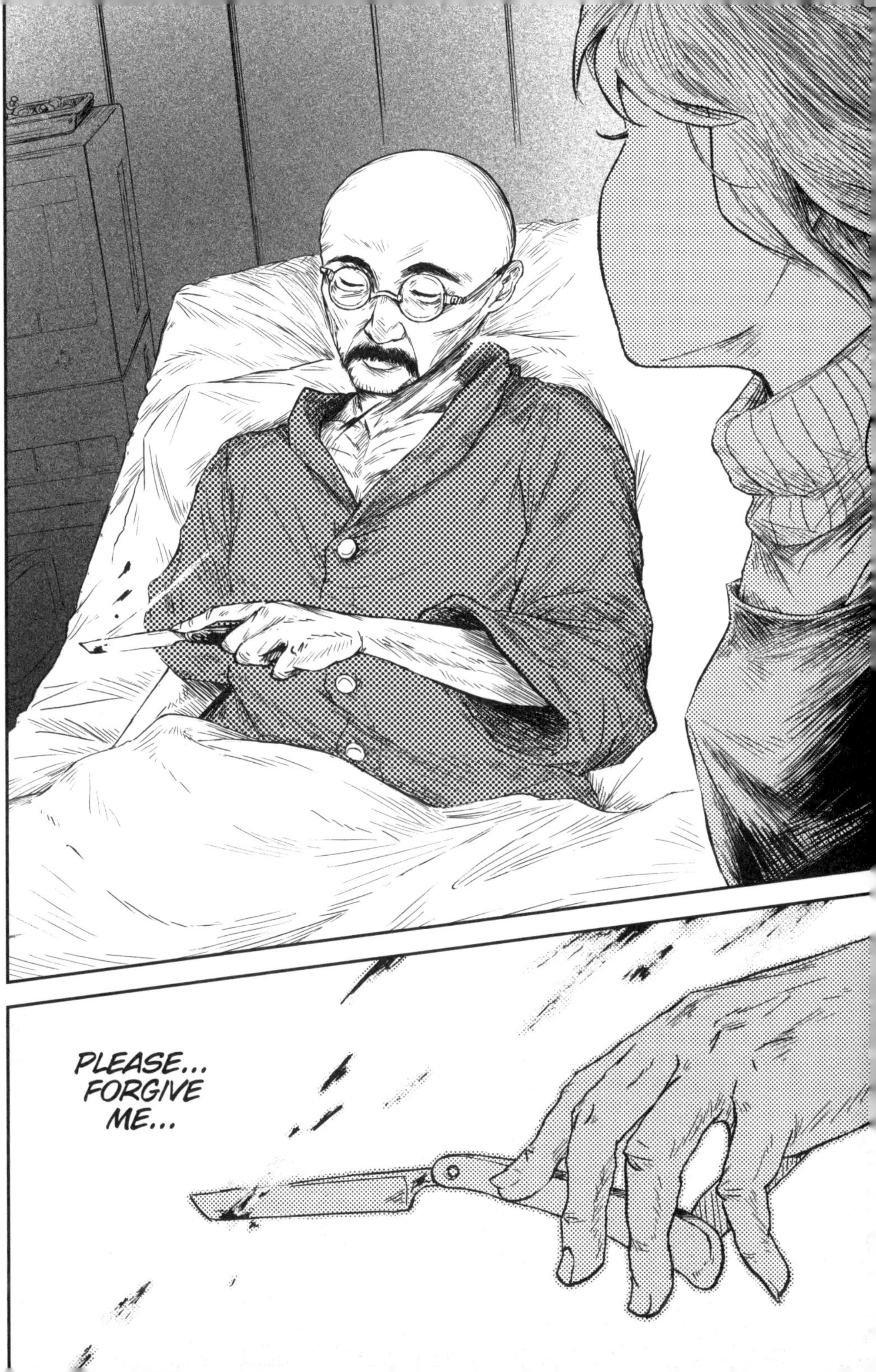
PLEASE...
FORGIVE
ME...

FORGIVE THIS FOOLISH FATHER...
FOR LEAVING ALL OF YOU BEHIND...
WH- WHY...

I'M SORRY, I TRICKED YOU...
THAT I USED YOU...
I'M SORRY, CHLOE...
NOW, EVERYTHING WILL BE OKAY...
NOW...
LEO CAN...
LEO CAN... LIVE...
CLATTER

AAUUUUUUGH!
DASH!
L-LEO... WAIT!
!

SLAM
Wait...
Leo! Wait!
Just wait!
Please!

FA-THER...
FA-THER...
L-LEO!
L-LISTEN TO ME...!
FATHER...
FA-THER!!

SLIP
THUD...

P-PLEASE...
J-JUST LISTEN TO ME...
I-I DIDN'T KNOW...
I NEVER THOUGHT ...
HE WOULD...
DO SOME-THING LIKE THAT...

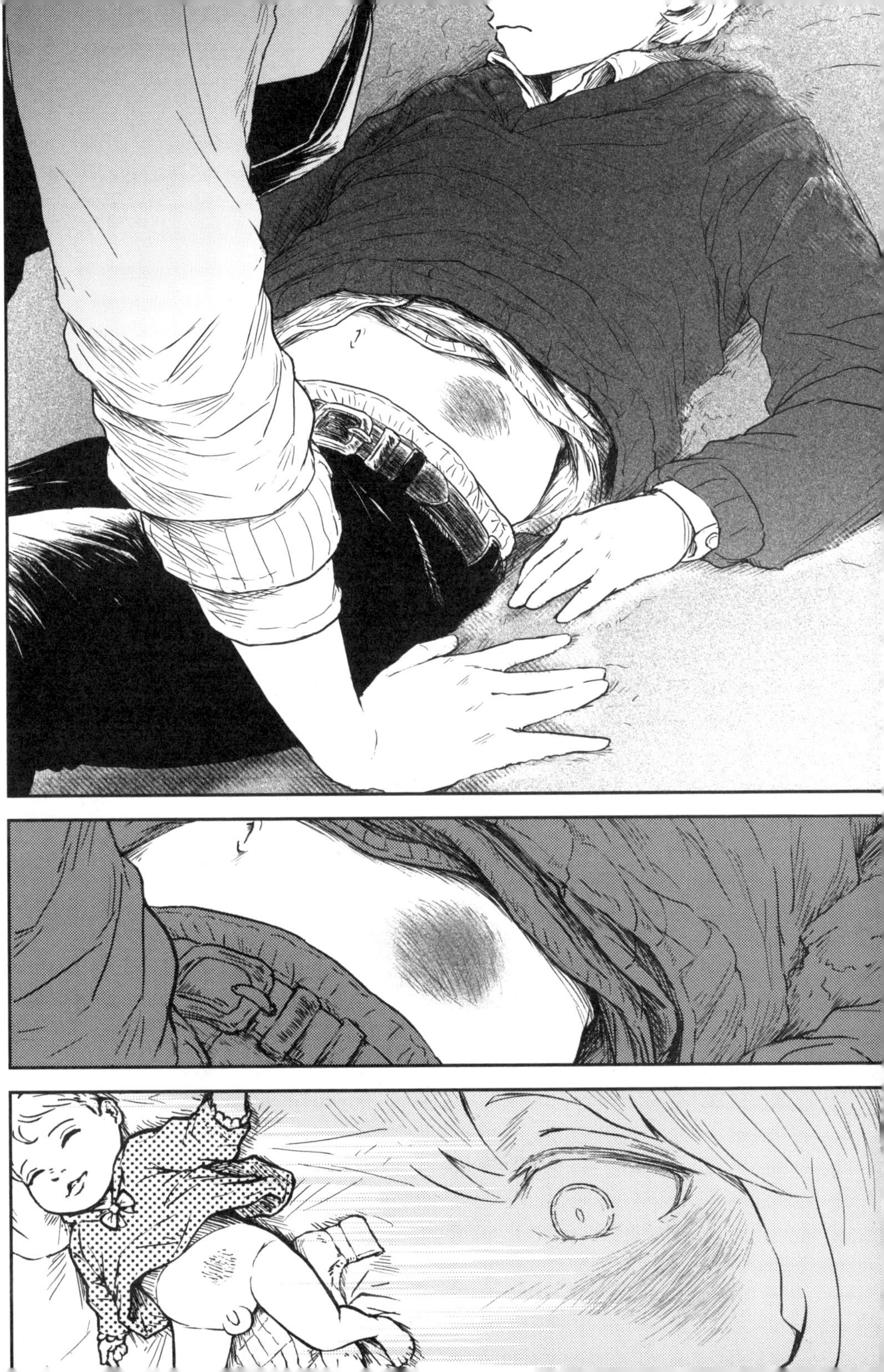

Chapter 11: Child of God

WHOOOSH
......

NO...
IT CAN'T BE...
Y-YOU'RE...
MUR-DERER...
HUH...?
MUR-DERER ...!

......!
N-NO...I DIDN'T...
STOP!
ARE YOU MAD?! DELTA INQUISITOR!
YOU MUST NOT GO ANY FURTHER!
THIS IS BLASPHEMY AGAINST GOD!
INQUISITOR, YOU HAVE NOT BEEN GRANTED PERMISSION TO SEE SERGEANT YOSHIKI!
SHUT YOUR TRAP! OUTTA MY WAY.
IT IS GOD'S WILL!

HMM...?
SOME-ONE'S THERE...
HANG ON...IS THAT...?
...?
SLIP
A...
F...
Fe...
Fem...
Female...

I'M....SO GRATE-FUL...
KLINK
KLINK
IT'S A GIFT...
ZSH
ZSH
ZSH
ZSH
ZSH
ZSH
FROM GOD!
I HAVE TO...
PROTECT HIM...
Sst...!

ZOON
ZOON
ZOON
HAH HAH ...!
PLIP

GRIP
THIS GIRL...
COULD SHE BE...?
STOP IT.

DON'T LAY A HAND ON HER.
TCH...!

MY WORD IS ABSOLUTE, REMEMBER?
DON'T YOU DARE LAY A SINGLE FINGER ON HER!
SWIP
SILENCE

THAT'S THE KID FROM OL' MAN YOSHIKI'S PLACE...
SCRATCH
WHAT A PAIN...
......
L-LORD LEO...
HIS HOLINESS THE POPE HAS CALLED ON LORD YOSHIKI...
HE INQUIRES AFTER THE STATE OF NOAH'S ARK.
......
MY FATHER... IS BUSY RIGHT NOW...
SO, ON AN-OTHER DAY...
SNATCH
WE CAN'T ALLOW THAT.
DO WHAT YOU MUST TO SEE THAT HE COMES.
AS "ABSO-LUTE" AS YOUR WORD IS...
SO ARE THE ORDERS OF HIS HOLINESS THE POPE.
......

I'LL GO...
I'LL BE THE ONE TO REPORT ON THE ARK'S PROGRESS.
...??!
TAKE ME TO THE POPE.
LOOM!
WE'LL TAKE 'EM THERE.
KOBA-YASHI, GIVE THE KID A LIFT.
PAT!
EH? S-SURE.
WE SHALL ACCOMPANY YOU THERE.

I'M FINE... DON'T FOLLOW ME.
L-LEO...
CRUNCH
CRUNCH...
......!
GO BACK...
AND CLEAN FATHER...

CRUNCH!
CRUNCH!
CRUNCH!
......
DELTA, YOU BACKED DOWN PRETTY EASILY, DIDN'CHA?
JUST WHEN I THOUGHT YOU WERE GONNA BULLDOZE YOUR WAY THROUGH.
......
I THINK... I'M IN LOVE.
EH?
WHEN YOU GET TO MY LEVEL, YOU CAN SENSE THE REAL DEAL AT A GLANCE.
THAT GIRL...
SHE CAN KICK SOME REAL ASS.

CLUNK
Journal
Journal

How did baby survive the fall?
Speculation Diaper filled with air
Maybe the diaper expanded with air underneath his clothes, serving as a kind of parachute
Proof: only the diaper was torn up
Also, since babies have soft, flexible bodies, maybe the muscles didn't tense upon impact, which mitigated the damage.
Notes
Torn diaper
Leo 0 years 6 months? Male
Leg: Fracture/Treated
Frostbite/Recovered
Personality: gentle, quiet. Stopped crying after wounds were treated. Eats well.
Repeats the word "sissy" when communicating
some reason.
A CHILD'S POSSIBILITIES ARE INFINITE.

DEPENDING ON THEIR EDUCATOR, THEY MAY GROW TO BE GOOD, OR EVIL.
THEY COULD BECOME A DOCTOR, AN ENGINEER, OR EVEN A RULER...
THEY ARE AN EXISTENCE WITH UNLIMITED POTENTIAL...
Look! A baby!
It's still alive!
What...?! How's that possible?
It fell down from the wall and survived?!
Let me pass...
!
Your holiness...!

Truly, God's fallen child.
Soon, it will draw its final breath...
This is a blessing bestowed upon us by God.
Let us gratefully accept the miracle of this life.
Wait.
I'll take that child under my wing.

Ser-geant Yoshi-ki...
As you well know...
in our faith, we devour those poor souls who cannot survive...
and live with them inside of us.
This child shall not die a dog's death.
Rather, its soul shall transcend to the sublime.
And yet...
you ask me to steal that blessing from this child and hand it over...
to you?
Don't be pompous with me.
You shouldn't lose sight of your own goal.

You're the ones who need an ark to escape this prison, aren't you?
In order to construct my ark, I need a human that I can mold.
If I teach this child from his infancy, he will comprehend my knowledge and learn to draw out a complete blueprint.
By the time I'm at death's door, that child will be able to provide you with your ark.
Besides... there's also your promise to me.
You promised not to lay your hands on the factory children.

Your faith is noth-ing but a scam anyway.
Don't you think my opinion should be given priority?
What a horrible thing to say...
Well...I guess this child's situation is just so irregular...
it makes even *me* want to believe in God...
He could truly be...
a mi-raculous child...
Very well...

I'll let you have it.
Honestly, I don't have a taste for babies.
Raise this child to be beautiful and intelligent, just the way I like them.

It's around twelve or thirteen... I'd say...
when they start to look the most delicious.
I won't be able to wait any longer than that.
WITHIN THE CONSTRAINTS OF MY PROMISE WITH THE POPE, I GAVE LEO A SPECIAL EDUCATION.
DEPENDING ON HOW YOU LOOK AT IT, THE KNOWLEDGE I PASSED ON WAS ONLY A TEMPORARY FIX...
HOWEVER, I STILL BELIEVE.

LEO.
YOU WILL BECOME A RAY OF HOPE FOR THE OTHER CHILDREN.
I WANT YOU TO DO WHATEVER YOU CAN TO GUIDE THESE SMALL LIVES.

CRUNCH...!

THEY'RE THE KIDS FROM THE FACTORY.
THEY'RE ALL FORCED TO WORK AT THE POPE'S FACTORY.
BUT YA KNOW...
WE'RE NOT NECESSAR-ILY SLAVES THERE.
OLD MAN YOSHIKI MADE SURE TO EDUCATE EVERY ONE OF US AND TEACH US VALUABLE SKILLS...
SO THAT NONE OF THEM WOULD LAY A HAND ON US.
THAT'S HOW...
THE OL' MAN PROTECTED US...

SLAM...
CHLOE...
DON'T BLAME YOURSELF SO MUCH.
OLD MAN YOSHIKI HAD BEEN LIKE THAT FOR SOME TIME NOW.
IT'S NOT YOUR FAULT, YA KNOW.
......!
WE SHOULD'VE BEEN UP FRONT AND TOLD YOU INSTEAD OF HIDING IT...
WELL, AT LEAST TRY TO STAY OUT OF LEO'S WAY.
THAT KID REALLY WAS A DADDY'S BOY...
BIG BROTHER LEO.
BADUM...!
Speak of the devil...

LEO...
WE JUST NEEDED...
A LITTLE MORE TIME...
THEN FATHER AND ALL OF US COULD'VE GOTTEN OUT OF THIS CITY ON THE ARK.
IF ONLY...
IF ONLY YOU HADN'T COME!
GET OUT!

LEO! DON'T BLAME THIS ON CHLOE.
YOU SHOULD'VE EXPECTED THAT FROM OLD MAN YOSHIKI.
I TOLD YOU! I TOLD YOU NOT TO TAKE OFF HIS HANDCUFFS!
BUT YOU...
BUT YOU DIDN'T LISTEN AND DID IT ANYWAY!
NOW I KNOW ...!
I SHOULD'VE LISTENED TO MY FATHER'S WARNING.
I SHOULDN'T HAVE LET ANY STRANGERS INTO OUR HOUSE!
I-I CAN'T EVEN STAND TO BE NEAR YOU...!

IT'S NOT...
CHLOE'S FAULT.
CHLOE...
WON'T GO ANY-WHERE.

IF I LOST MY SISTER TOO...
IT WOULD BE...TOO MUCH FOR ME...
CLACK...!

CLACK
CLACK
CLACK
CLACK
......
I GOTTA DO SOME-THING...

SPLISH
SPLISH
SPLISH
SPLISH
LEO AND SEBASTIAN, IT'S YOUR FIRST TIME PASSING THROUGH THIS WAY, RIGHT?
AT THIS POINT, WE'VE ALREADY ENTERED THE NEIGHBORING DISTRICT.
UNDERGROUND IT'S ONLY ONE STRAIGHT PATH, SO YOU CAN GET HERE IN A JIFFY.
THIS DISTRICT IS ALSO UNDER THE POPE'S JURISDICTION, BUT...
glance!
......

THERE'S A PLACE HERE THAT ONLY I KNOW ABOUT.
I'M GONNA OPEN THIS SHUTTER, SO HANG ON A SEC.
CHLOE, GIMME A HAND.
Oof
CHLOE.
I'M GONNA NEED YOU TO PUT IN EXTRA EFFORT TODAY.
YEAH?
HUH?
SURE...
AND NOW...
LET THE SHOW BEGIN!
KLANG

MUSIC HALL
FREDLIC
W-WHOA! I SAW THIS IN A BOOK ONCE!
IT'S A MOOOVIE THEATER!

FLAP!
WE'RE THE ONLY ONES WHO KNOW ABOUT THIS PLACE.
ALMOST, BUT NOT QUITE.
THIS IS A MUSICAL THEATER.
THE PART ABOVE GROUND WAS DESTROYED, BUT I GUESS THAT WAS LUCKY...
'CAUSE NOW THOSE GUYS CAN'T GET IN HERE.
CLICK!
ON
OFF
MUSIC HALL
FREDLIC
IN THE OLD DAYS, PEOPLE USED TO DANCE...
TO DISTRACT THEMSELVES FROM THEIR PAIN AND SORROW.

WHICH MEANS THAT WHAT WE NEED RIGHT NOW IS TO DANCE!
Cough!
...
??!
WH- WHAT ...?!
YOUR HAND, M'LADY.
I-I DON'T KNOW HOW TO DANCE EITHER, BUT...
IF WE HOLD HANDS AND DO SOME STEPS, IT SHOULD LOOK LIKE WE'RE DANCING.

LET'S GIVE IT A TRY.
TO EN-COURAGE LEO AS WELL.
SURE.
Three.
One.
Two.
Three.
Two.
One.

"LEO..."
W-WOULD YOU...L-LIKE TO JOIN ME...IF-IF YOU DON'T MIND...?

I'M A TERRIBLE DANCER...
......
OF COURSE NOT...
AND I'VE GOT A BAD LEG.
BUT IF THAT DOESN'T BOTHER YOU...

THE TRUTH IS, I KNEW ALL ALONG...
tear...
THAT FATHER... INTENDED TO DIE...
THAT'S WHAT HE'S ALWAYS TOLD ME.

HE TOLD ME THAT HE WAS GOING TO DIE IN THIS CITY...
SO I NEEDED TO ESCAPE AND FIND MY REAL FAMILY.
BUT I COULDN'T BEAR IT...
AND SHACKLED HIM UP... AGAINST HIS WILL...
I KNEW ALL ALONG...
BUT I STILL... SAID THOSE AWFUL THINGS TO YOU...
I'M SORRY...
THAT I CALLED YOU A MURDER-ER...
SOR-RY...
SLIP...!

HUSH...
BZZT!
slip!
sniff
JUST WHEN IT WAS GETTING GOOD...
TH-THAT HUNK OF JUNK...!
I GUESS... I KINDA BARED MY SOUL A BIT THERE, HUH...?
I'M ALWAYS OFF MY GUARD WITH YOU...
I CAN REALLY UNDER-STAND...
WHY SEBASTIAN CALLS YOU SISTER...

I'D SURE BE HAPPY IF I HAD A SISTER TOO...
I...
I'M YOUR...
I HAD A LOT OF FUN TODAY...

LET'S DANCE TOGETHER AGAIN SOMEDAY.
NEXT TIME YOUR LITTLE BROTHER CAN JOIN US TOO.
LEO.

F-
FOR...
SO,
SO...
SO
LONG...
I'VE
WANTED...
W-
WANTED
TO SEE
Y-Y...

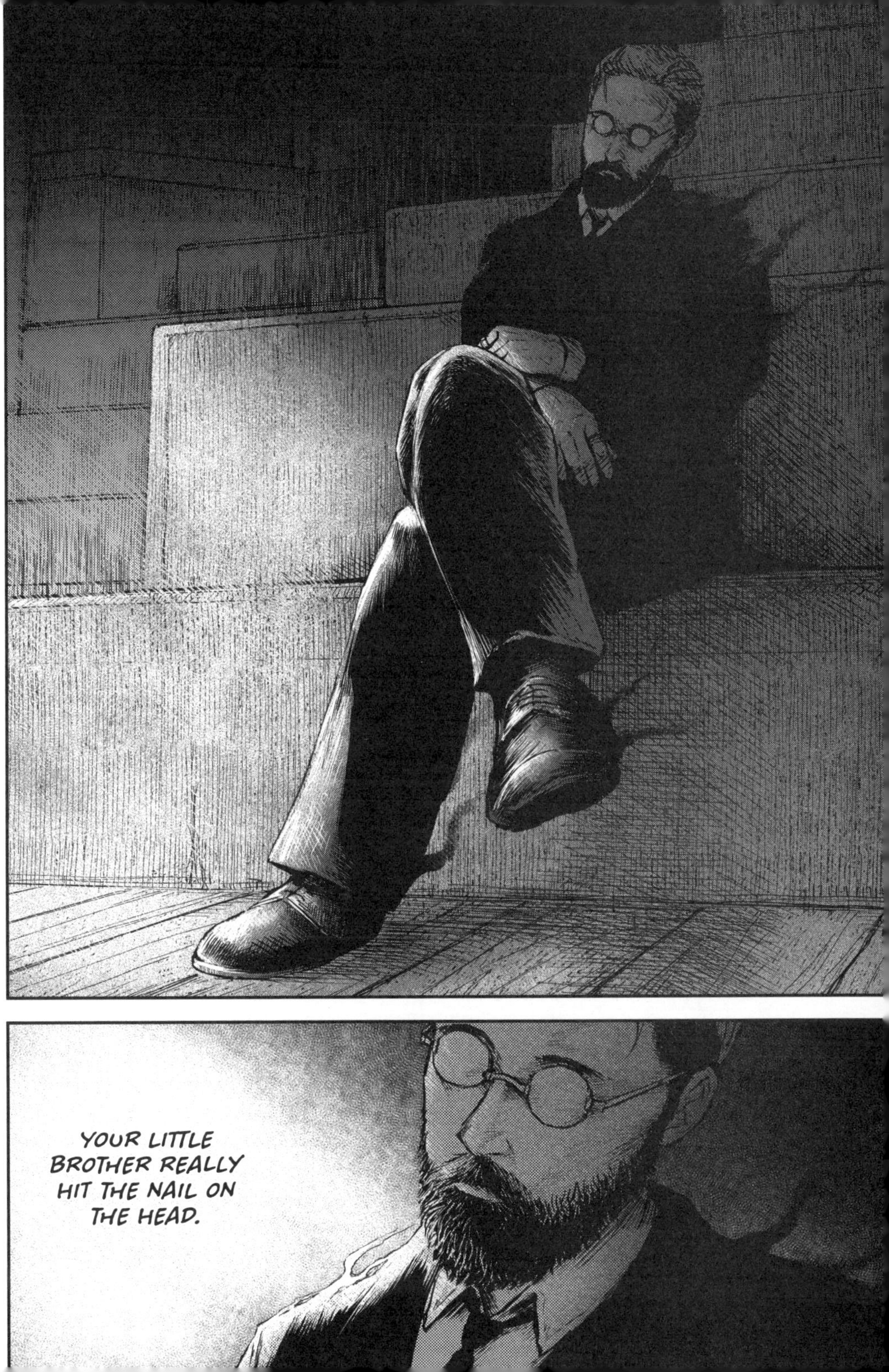
YOUR LITTLE BROTHER REALLY HIT THE NAIL ON THE HEAD.

A MURDERER, THAT'S WHAT YOU ARE.
NO MATTER HOW YOU TO TRY TO FORGET...
THE TRUTH CANNOT BE DENIED.
HAVE A LOOK BEHIND YOU.

THE PATH YOU'VE TRODDEN IS LITTERED WITH CORPSES.

THE VERY SAME HANDS YOU EMBRACED LOCKE WITH ARE STAINED CRIMSON WITH BLOOD...
YOUR BROTHER WAS NOT MISTAKEN WHEN HE CALLED YOU A MURDERER...
NEVER-THELESS...
"IT WAS ALL FOR YOU.
"I'VE COME BACK ALL THIS WAY JUST TO HOLD YOUR HAND ONCE MORE..." SAY IT.
NOW...
TELL HIM.

THAT YOU ARE HIS SISTER...
WHO DIRTIED HER HANDS WITH BLOOD, ALL IN HIS NAME.

......?
THAT DOESN'T CHANGE THE FACT THAT I HURT YOU...
BUT... IF YOU'LL ALLOW ME TO ATONE FOR MY SIN...
BY YOUR SIDE...
THEN I HOPE YOU'LL ALSO ALLOW ME TO HELP YOU WITH WHAT YOU WANT TO ACCOMPLISH...

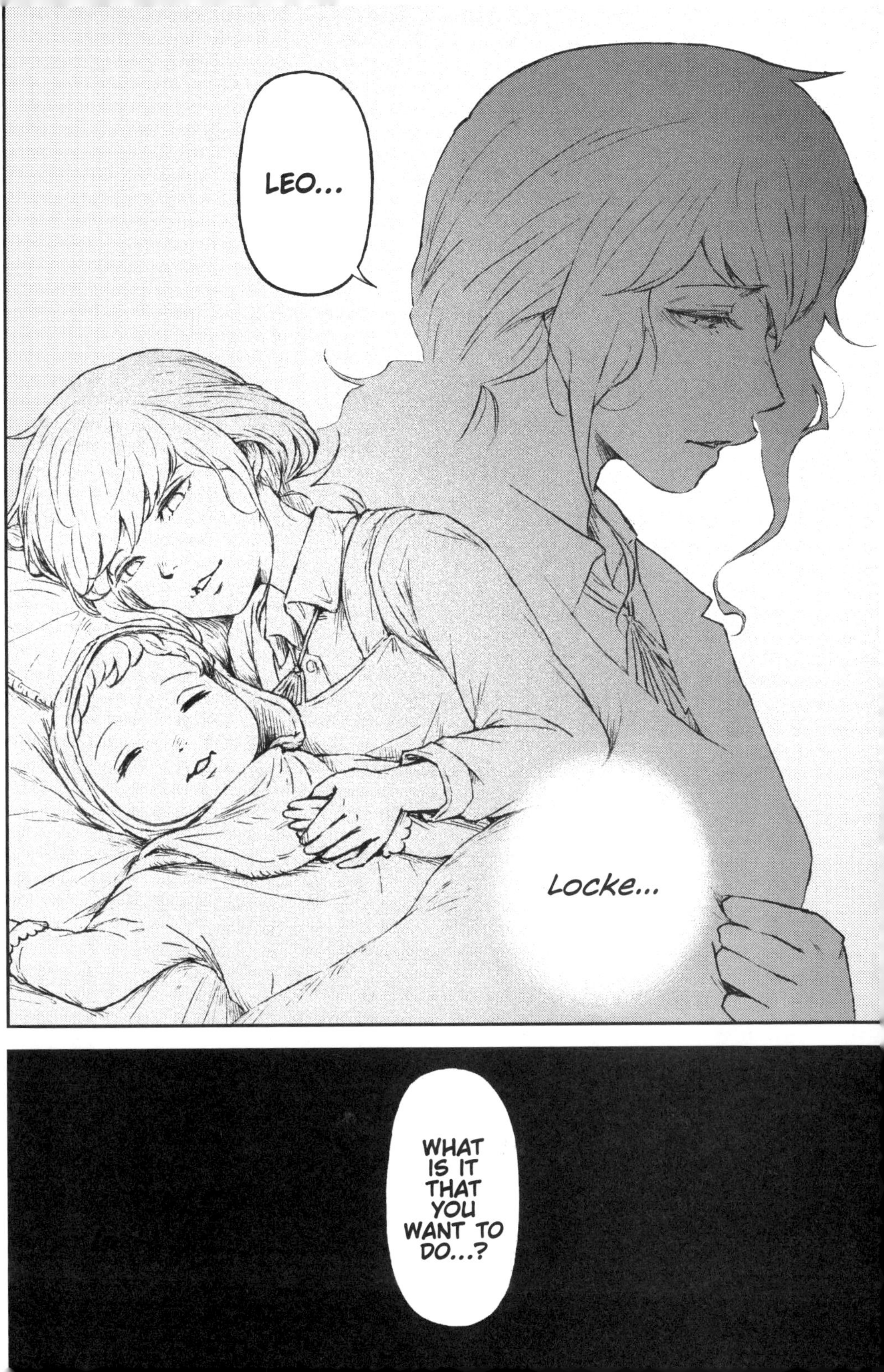
LEO...
Locke...
WHAT IS IT THAT YOU WANT TO DO...?

Shuff
Shuff

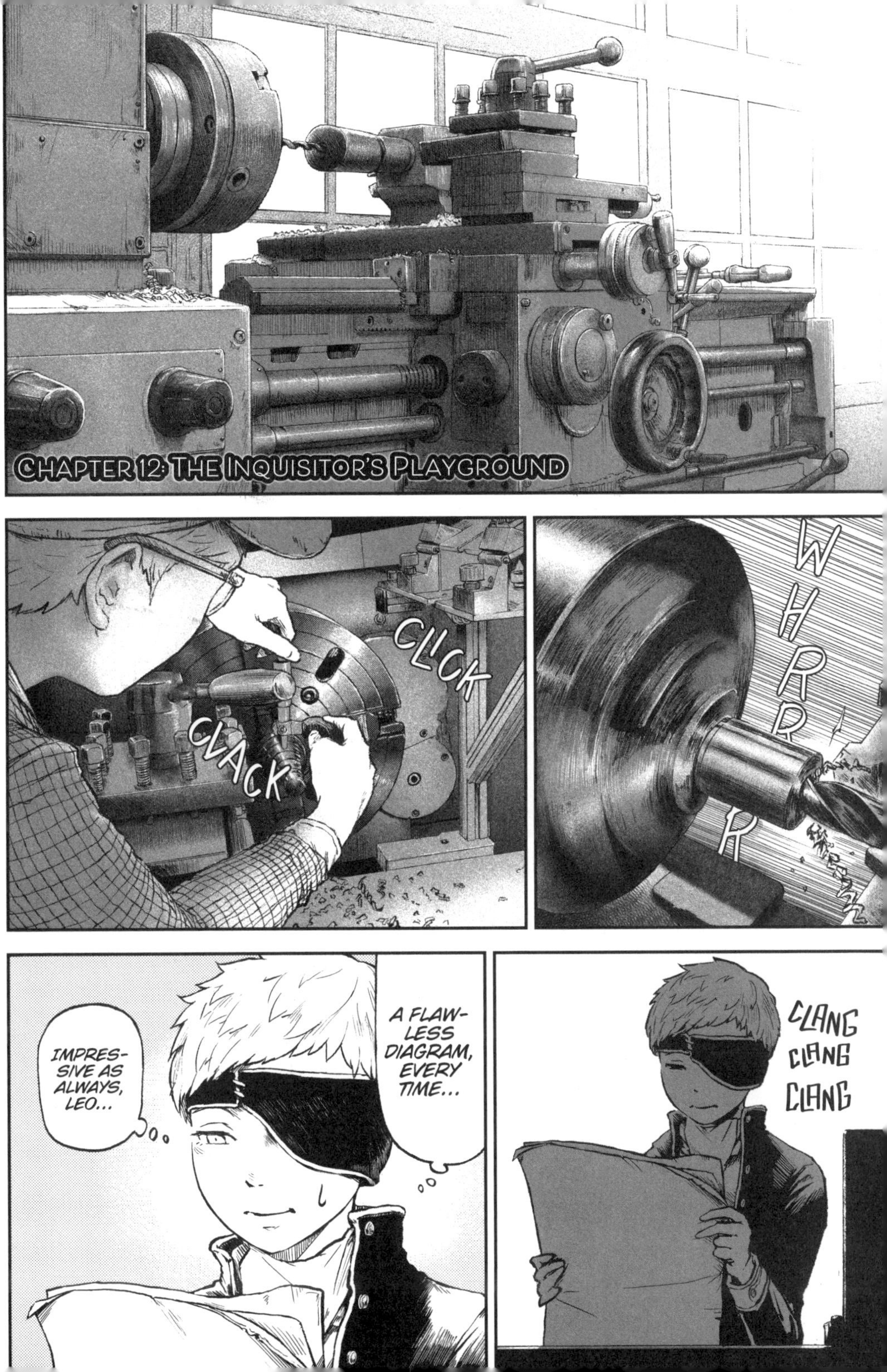
Chapter 12: The Inquisitor's Playground
CLICK
CLACK
WHRRRR
CLANG
CLANG
CLANG
A FLAW-LESS DIAGRAM, EVERY TIME...
IMPRES-SIVE AS ALWAYS, LEO...

WHAT'RE YOU LOOKIN' AT, BRAT?!
YOU'D BETTER FINISH TODAY'S WORK QUICK OR WE'LL GOBBLE YOU UP!
GA HA HA HA!
HMPH, THOSE DUMMIES DON'T EVEN KNOW WHAT WE'RE MAKING HERE.

GINA.
DON'T YOU DARE THINK WE'RE GONNA TAKE THIS FOREVER...
I GOT A MESSAGE FROM KEITH.
EACH GROUP LEADER IS TO GATHER IN THE MEETING ROOM.
LEO IS GOING TO VISIT OUR HOUSE.
...!
THE DAY SERGEANT YOSHIKI DIED...
FINALLY, HE'S MAKING A MOVE...

Thanks for coming Leo. How many years has it been since our last meeting, I wonder.

It almost makes me want to reminisce about old times...
but let's get down to business, shall we? Tell me about the ark.
According to Sergeant Yoshiki's promise to me, it should be finished this year, correct?
We can complete it in the next two months.
But we don't have the fuel that you're supposed to supply us with.
In order to make full use of the engine, we need ultonium.
Ah, how could I forget.
Although, even with my power, it's quite difficult to get my hands on a large quantity of ultonium...
Actually, that would be a difficult order to fulfill even outside of Prison City.
Is it ab-solutely neces-sary?
If we can't produce maximum output when escaping the city, we won't be able to scatter the guards.
After that, we can switch to solar energy and somehow manage to fly off...
but until then, it's definitely neces-sary.

I see... well, if I have two months, I'll get it somehow.
Thank you for being honest with me about the ark.
If we're done talking, I'm going home.
Don't rush off like that, it's been too long.
Let's have a little chat.
TAP!
I know!
I'll have you attend my sermon in two weeks' time.
I'd love for you to see me speak up close.
And the over-whelming number of devotees who will gather to hear me.
When you see that, you'll be reassured of my greatness.
I get it, so I'm leaving. Pick me up.
......
Oh...

Yoshiki died, didn't he?
I knew it.
Now I understand your hurry to leave...

When one lives as long as I, it becomes possible to see a person's death.
He and I knew each other for a long time, so this saddens me.
I'm leaving.
......
Leo.
If it pleases you, you can live here with me.
Along with all your friends, of course...
I promise not to mis-treat you...

SMACK!
Don't touch me!

I refuse to accept charity from you and your lot!
Heh...
Heh heh...
Eh heh heh...

Good boy... I'm pleased with you...
I was right to leave you in Yoshiki's care...
......
Finally, the time has come...
How many years has it been since we've seen the free world?
We hafta show our gratitude to those brats.
......

TOO BAD FOR THEM.
NO MATTER HOW GRATEFUL THEY MAY BE...
WE DON'T HAVE EVEN THE SLIGHTEST INTENTION OF LETTING THEM HITCH A RIDE WITH US.
THEY'RE SADLY MISTAKEN IF THEY THINK WE'RE JUST GONNA SHUT UP...
AND OBEDIENTLY LISTEN TO EVERYTHING WE'RE TOLD.
THEY'RE NOT THE ONES WHO'LL BE ESCAPING FROM THIS CITY.
IT'LL BE JUST US KIDS.
SO...
YOU'RE SAYING THAT YOU MANAGED TO FOOL THE POPE AND THE OTHERS?
THE ARK IS READY TO FLY AS SOON AS IT HAS THE NECESSARY ENERGY SOURCE.
BUT IT'S THE ENERGY SOURCE THAT'S THE THORN IN OUR SIDE... WHEN IT COMES TO ULTONIUM...
THERE'S NO CHANCE WE CAN GET ANY.
EVEN WITH THE ARK COMPLETED, WE WON'T BE ABLE TO MOVE IT.

THE POPE BELIEVES THAT WE CAN'T GATHER ENOUGH ENERGY ON OUR OWN.
LETTING THEM THINK THAT IS ALSO ONE OF OUR STRATEGIES.
YOU SHOULD ALL BE PRETTY FAMILIAR WITH SOMETHING IN THIS CITY THAT'S POWERED BY ULTONIUM.
YEP.
FROM WHAT YOU'RE SAYING, IT SOUNDS LIKE WE CAN GET OUR HANDS ON ULTONIUM OURSELVES.
WHAT DO YOU MEAN?
POWERED... BY ULTO-NIUM?
NO WAY...!
...!

THE GUARDS?!
YEP.
THOSE GUYS ARE POWERED BY A NUCLEAR REACTOR.
EVEN A SINGLE UNIT CARRIES AN INCREDIBLE AMOUNT OF ENERGY.
OF COURSE, OBTAINING IT WON'T EXACTLY BE A PIECE OF CAKE...
THAT'S TOO RECK-LESS!
YOU GOTTA BE CRAZY TO THINK THAT THE LIKES OF US HAVE ANY CHANCE AGAINST THOSE MON-STERS.
BESIDES, L-LET'S JUST SAY WE MANAGE TO GET ONE OF 'EM. THAT STILL WOULDN'T BE ENOUGH TO MOVE THE ARK.
NO MATTER HOW PURE THEIR ENERGY MAY BE...
WAIT.
I GET IT NOW...

THERE'S A MOUNTAIN OF GUARD UNITS THERE THAT DELTA AND THE OTHERS HAVE DESTROYED!
!
THE INQUISI-TORS' PLAY-GROUND!
BUT...HOW'RE WE SUPPOSED TO GET TO A DANGEROUS PLACE LIKE THAT...?
YOU CAN LEAVE THAT TO US!
THE LEMMING BROTH-ERS.
UNLIKE YOU GUYS, WE DON'T GOT ANY SPECIAL SKILLS OR KNOWLEDGE.
BUT THIS IS SUMMIN' WE CAN DO.

IT'S A VERY DANGER-OUS TASK.
BUT SOMEONE'S GOTTA DO IT, RIGHT?
WE WANNA CON-TRIBUTE SUMMIN'. LET US DO IT, WOULD YA?
......
THE LEMMING BROTHERS ARE RIGHT.
I'LL GO WITH THEM.
I'M OLDER, AND I'M A DECENT JUDGE OF THINGS.
PLUS...I'M EVERYONE'S LEADER, YOU KNOW?
...!

I CAN'T STRESS ENOUGH THAT THIS IS WAY TOO DANGER-OUS...
IF WE'RE BUSTED FOR SNEAKING INTO THE INQUISITORS' AREA...
WE'RE ALREADY LIVING IN A CONSTANT STATE OF DANGER.
IF WE DON'T CLEAR THIS OB-STACLE IN OUR PATH...
WE'LL NEVER BE ABLE TO DECEIVE THE POPE.
WE'VE MANAGED THIS FAR.
IT'LL BE A WALK IN THE PARK.
shake

SO... YOU'RE CHLOE, AREN'T YOU?
I'M JEM.
THIS IS MY LITTLE BRO, DORY.
Oh... nice to meet you...
WE COULDN'T FORGET ABOUT YOU AFTER SEEING YOU AT MR. YOSHIKI'S FUNERAL.
WE HAVE A FAVOR TO ASK YOU.
WILL YOU LET US TOUCH YOUR BOOBIES?
BOO-BIES?
BOO-BIES.
BOO-BIES.
HEY!
THAT'S NOT SOMETHING YOU SAY TO A GIRL.
LOOK HOW UNCOMFORTABLE YOU'RE MAKING CHLOE!

DIDN'T MR. YOSHIKI TEACH YOU THAT YOU SHOULD BE POLITE TO GIRLS?
WHADDYA EXPECT!
YOU AND RABI WON'T LET US TOUCH 'EM.
OF COURSE WE WON'T!
......
THEY'RE JUST LITTLE KIDS, SO TRY TO FORGIVE THEM.
BUT IT'S NOT A GOOD IDEA TO DRESS SO OBVIOUSLY LIKE A GIRL.
YOU'VE GOTTA BE CAREFUL AND HIDE IT.
OH... YEAH...
CHLOE, RIGHT? I'M GINA.
THIS HERE IS RABIKO.
NICE TO MEET YOU.
YEAH... YOU TOO...
FROM WHAT KEITH SAYS...
YOU MADE IT HERE FROM THE FIRST DISTRICT ALL BY YOURSELF.
IS THAT TRUE?
Y-YEAH...I GUESS SO...
HMM...
YOU DON'T LOOK LIKE SUCH AN AMAZING FIGHTER, THOUGH...

......
LIS-TEN.
KEITH...
HE MAY PUT ON A COOL FACE IN FRONT OF EVERYONE, BUT...
THE TRUTH IS THAT HE'S PUSHING HIMSELF TO ACT THAT WAY.
CHLOE.
IF YOU REALLY ARE SUCH A SKILLED FIGHTER, THEN I WANT YOU TO BE THERE TO HELP HIM.
PAT!
JUST KIDDING!
I'LL JUST ASK THAT YOU PRAY FOR THEM...
THAT THEY'LL PULL THROUGH.

You're their leader...
and their big brother.
All the children here love you dearly.
With all of you together...
I'm sure that you can overcome any number of difficulties.

CLUNK...
However, in this city, you must have power...
in order to protect that bond.
Use this to protect your brothers and sisters.
Don't use it until then.

YEAH... THAT'S RIGHT...
THE TIME HAS COME FOR ME TO USE THIS, HASN'T IT, OL' MAN...?
I CAN DO THIS. I KNOW I CAN...
I'M THE BIG BROTH-ER...
EVERY-ONE'S BIG BROTHER!
I HAVE TO PRO-TECT THEM!

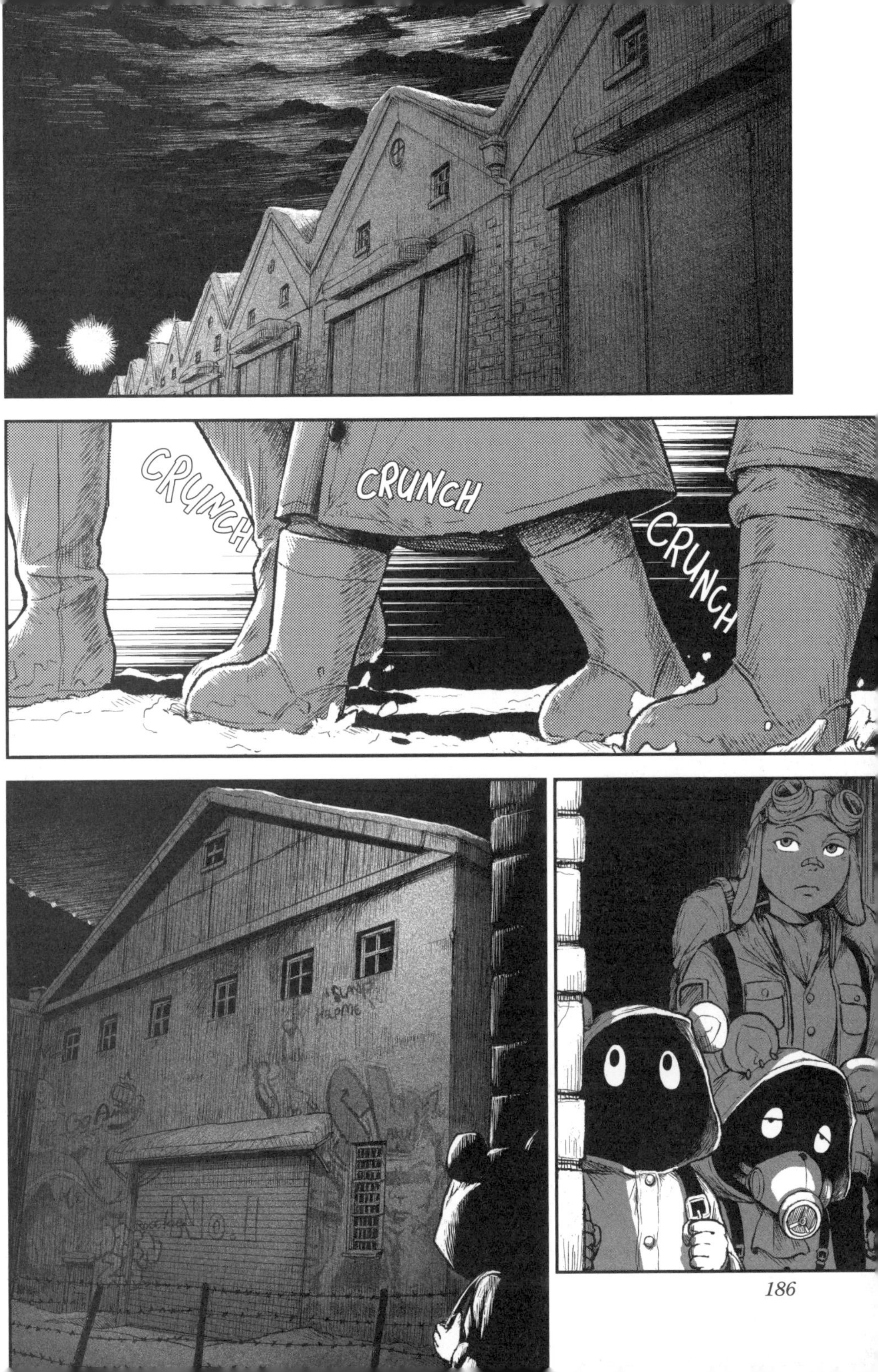
CRUNCH
CRUNCH
CRUNCH
No. 1

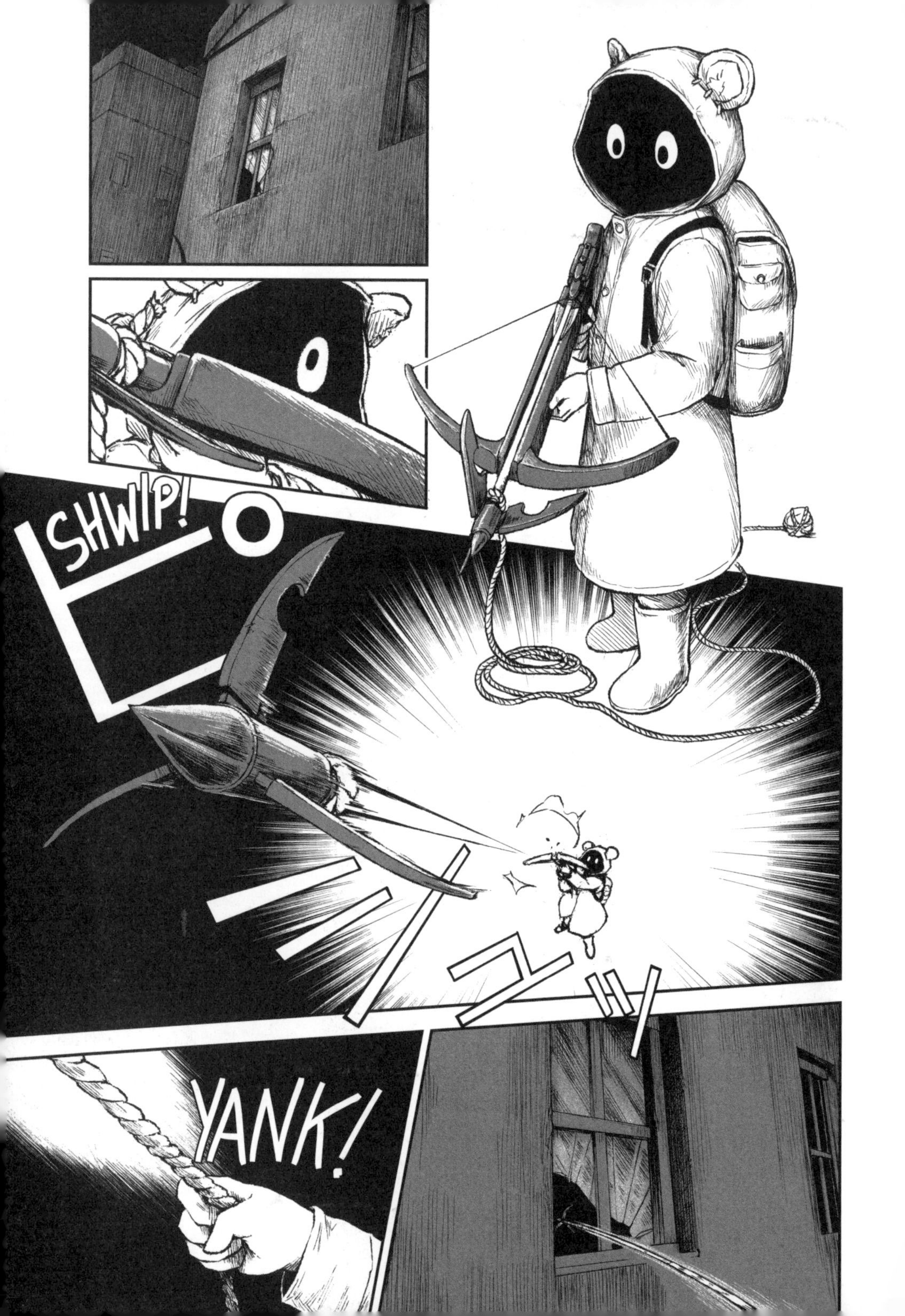
SHWIP!
YANK!

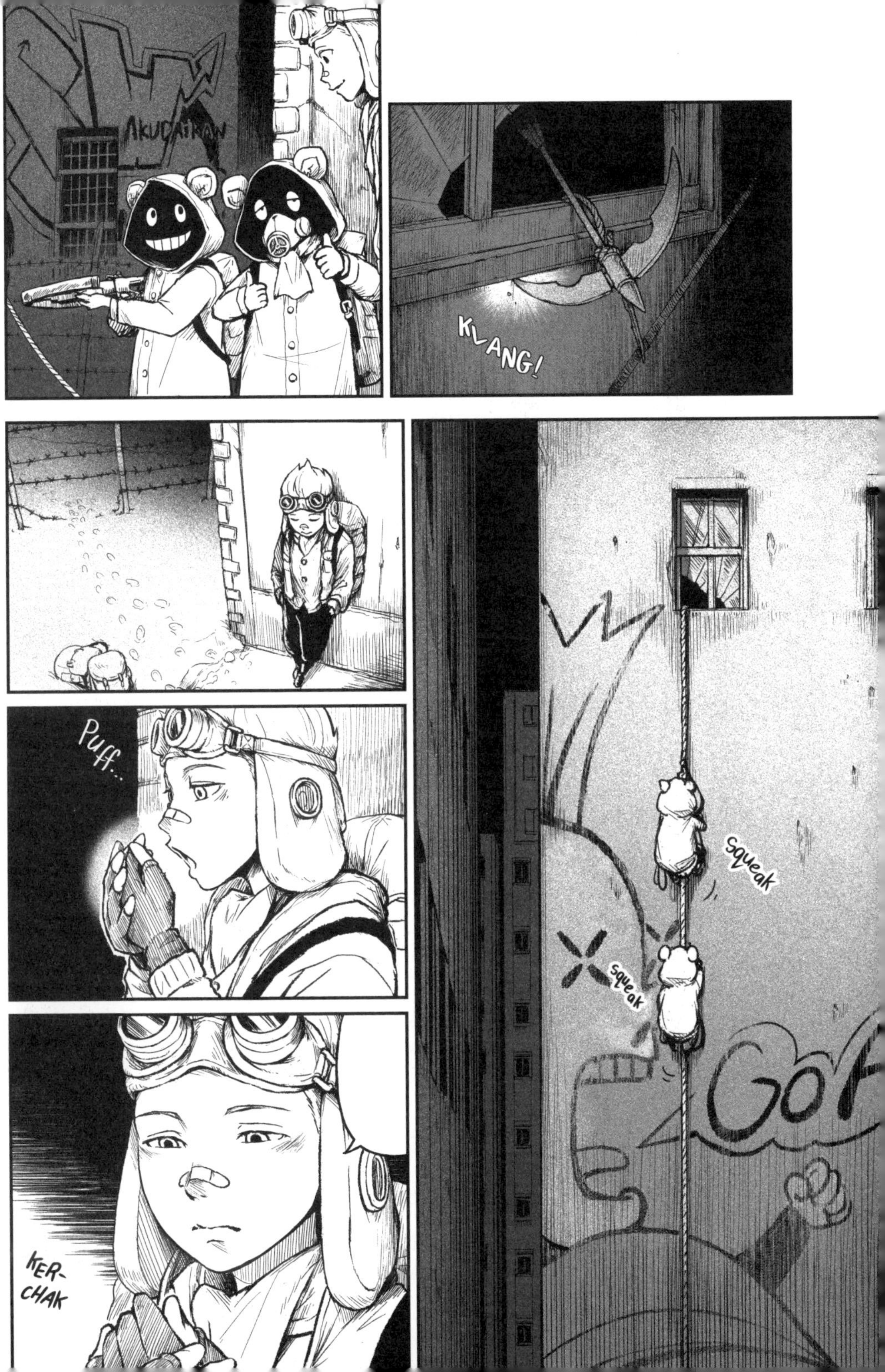

AKUDAIKAN
KLANG!
Puff...
KER-
CHAK
squeak
squeak
GO

CLICK!

gulp...

YANK
YANK...
RRRIP...
LET'S TAKE AS MANY AS WE CAN CARRY...
......

FLASH!

BOOM
BOOM
SCRATCH
BOOM
BWOOM
BWOOM
BWOOM
BWOOM
KSH

LOOOM
YO, YO, LI'L MICE...
WHAT ARE YA SCRATCHIN' AROUND FOR IN HERE...?

HEH HEH HEH...
SNIFF...
THERE'S NO POINT IN HIDIN' NOW!
THE NAME'S HUNGER!
THERE'S NO OTHER IN THIS WORLD WITH A NOSE TO MATCH MINE!
I CAN TELL EXACTLY WHERE YOU ARE FROM YOUR FOUL SMELL ALONE!
Child Killer Hunger
EVEN GOD'S CHILDREN ARE BANNED FROM SNEAKIN' INTO OUR HIDEOUT HERE!
AND IF ANYONE BREAKS THE RULES...

BAM!!
THAT MEANS WE CAN GOBBLE 'EM UP!
SHING...!
THIS IS FANTAS-TIC...
IT'S BEEN TOO LONG SINCE I'VE HAD A BITE OF A CHILD'S FLESH.
RATTLE
WH-WH-WHAT SHOULD WE DO...?
WHY'D THE MEANEST-LOOKIN' ONE HAVE TO FIND US?!

D-DON'T WORRY.
I-I...
I'LL PROTECT US.
THE SMELL OF A GUN CARTRIDGE...
HEH HEH. GIVE IT UP ALREADY.
USING THAT THING IN YOUR CURRENT MENTAL STATE...
YOU WON'T BE HITTIN' NOTHIN'!
OL' MAN...
IS THIS WHERE YOU'RE HIDIN'...?
G-SHK!
OR ARE YA OVER HERE?
YOU ALWAYS PROTECTED US...
GRP!
WAIT A MINUTE... HERE YOU ARE!
AND I'VE CARRIED ON YOUR WILL!
NOW IT'S MY TURN TO...

PROTECT EVERYONE!
CRACK!
FFT...!
...!

...?!
COME OUT AND SHOW YOURSELF!
WHO DID THAT?! WHO'S THE BASTARD THAT BROKE THE LIGHT?!
LET'S GET OUT WHILE WE STILL HAVE THE CHANCE!
I-I DUNNO WHAT'S GOING ON, BUT THIS IS OUR OPPORTUNITY.
...?
DASH!
EH?
SNEAK...!
FWOOSH
YOU AIN'T GETTING' AWAY!

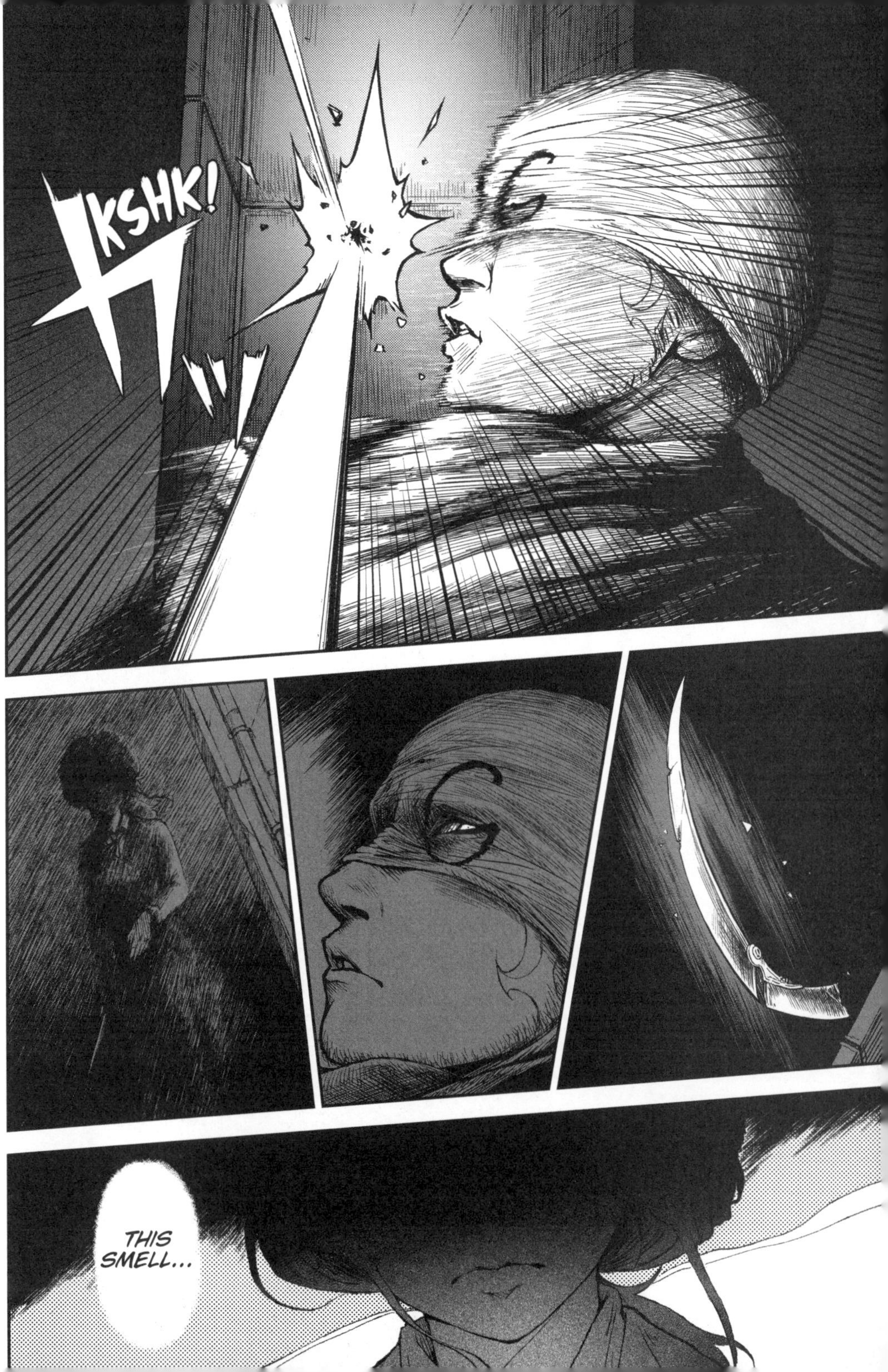
KSHK!
THIS SMELL...

GG
IT'S THE SAME GIRL FROM BACK THEN!

HMPH... SEEMS LIKE YOU GOT PRETTY GOOD EYES.
AND IF YOU'RE STILL HERE, YOU MUST HAVE A LOTTA CONFIDENCE IN YOUR SKILLS...
YO.
GIMME ALL THE SMOKE YOU GOT.

POOF!
FSSSS

HEH HEH HEH... YOU SHOULD BE HAPPY.
Sniff
THE STAGE IS SET, JUST FOR YOU.
ISN'T IT PERFECT FOR A DANCE?

HMM... HE HASN'T COME BY HERE.
STRANGE THAT THE COLONEL WOULD TAKE OFF SOMEWHERE WITHOUT SAYING ANYTHING.
OH...
HE NEVER DID THAT WHEN HE WAS IN THE ARMY.
CHAPTER 13: AWARENESS OF SIN

I DOUBT IT'S ANYTHING TO WORRY ABOUT, AT LEAST WHEN IT COMES TO HIM.
HE'LL PROBABLY WANDER BACK AT SOME POINT....
HMM... YOU'RE PROBABLY RIGHT.
DEAR!
I SAW THE COLONEL THE DAY BEFORE YESTERDAY.
THE COLONEL WAS PASSING THROUGH THE TICKET GATE AND HEADING TO THE PLATFORM AT THE TRAIN STATION.
WHICH PLATFORM WAS IT?
HMM...I THINK IT WAS THE ONE ON THE FAR SIDE.
......!
MIYAKO.

THE COLONEL MIGHT HAVE GONE TO THE NEIGH-BORING COUNTRY.
HE WOULDN'T ...!
MY FATHER IS AN A-RANK CRIMINAL IN THAT COUNTRY!
chuckle!
NOW I SEE...
MOTHER-ER...??
EXACTLY.

HE'S GOT SOMETHING OVER THERE THAT HE WORRIES ABOUT EVEN MORE THAN HIMSELF...
BWOOM!
BWOOM!
BWOOM
I GUESS EVERY-THING YOU DID BACK-FIRED...

SWIP
JINGLE...
BOOM!
SWISH

HEE HEE HEH...
WHAT A PITY.
POOF...

ARE YOU... REALLY THE GIRL WHO RAN AWAY IN A PANIC THAT DAY?
sniff
sniff
The scent of female...
I CAN'T SENSE ANY OF THE *FEAR* I FELT FROM YOU THAT TIME...
IT'S AS IF YOU'RE AN ENTIRELY DIFFERENT PERSON.
SEEMS LIKE SOMETHING'S CHANGED IN YOU AFTER MEETING THAT PACK OF BRATS.
NEVERTHELESS...YOU'RE STILL A GOOD WOMAN.
IT WOULD BE A WASTE TO EAT YOU UP.
HMMM, HOW ABOUT...
KWNG...

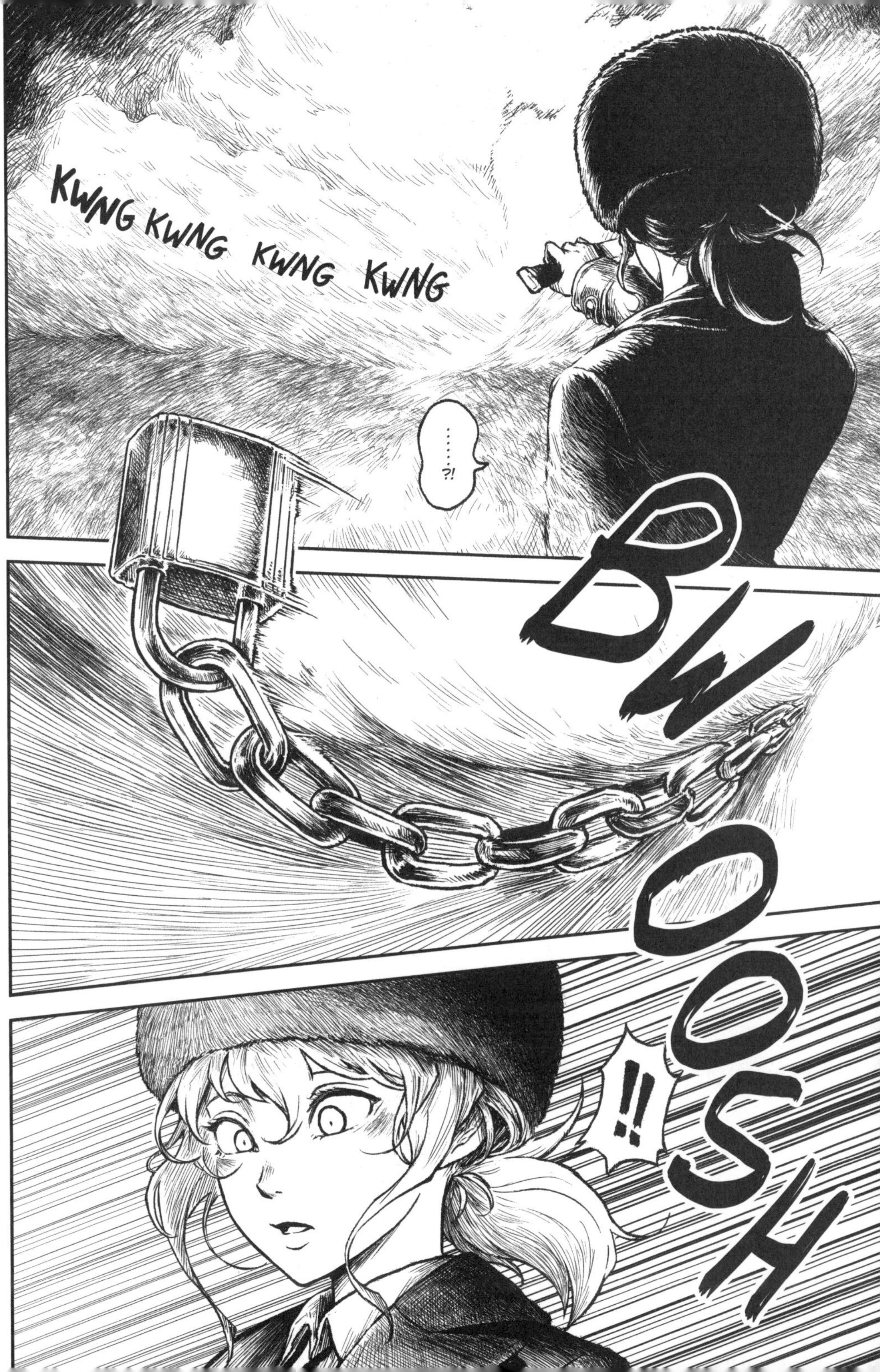
KWNG KWNG KWNG KWNG
......?!
BWOOOSH
!!

WHIP!
JANGLE
CLANG!

KWNG
SMIRK...

SST
UH-OH!
YANK!
!
DON'T BE MAKING ANY STUPID MOVES.
WHILE YOU'RE TRYING TO REMOVE THOSE CHAINS, MY KNIFE WILL SLICE RIGHT THROUGH YOUR FLESH.
......
GOOD GIRL.
YES... THAT'S RIGHT. DON'T MOVE A MUSCLE.
NO MATTER HOW VIOLENT, A LEOPARDESS IN A CAGE IS STILL AN ADORABLE SIGHT, DON'CHA THINK?
SO CUTE THAT I WANT TO DEVOUR HER.

FIRST HER EARS.
THEN HER EYES.
AND FINALLY, HER ARMS AND LEGS. SHE'LL BE NOTHING MORE THAN A PITIFUL PLAYTHING THEN.
BUT YA KNOW...
CARESS...
NO MATTER HOW BROKEN...
FWOOSH!

!
SNATCH!
I'LL LOVE YOU FOREVER, BABE.

CLINK...
GSH!
I'M BLOWN AWAY. YOU'RE A REAL BEAUTY...!
WHOA...
HOW VERY...
SLIP
SCRUMP-TIOUS YOU LOOK!
SHIVER

SCHK!
SLASH!
CRACK

WHAM!
YANK!
......
YOU REALLY ARE A GOOD WOMAN...

BE MINE.
THAT WAY YOU'LL ENJOY YOUR LIFE IN THIS CITY.
THE THING ABOUT WOMEN IS...
THEY'RE MADE FOR LOVIN' AND NOT FOR KILLIN'.

DON'T YOU... THINK SO, TOO?
WHAT'S THAT...?
......?

SEVEN...
SIX.
FIVE.
FOUR.
WHAT ...?
THREE.
TWO.
WHAT'RE YOU COUNTING DOWN--?
ONE.

HNG ...?

Augh!
Ah!
Ah!
CRASH
WHAT THE HELL'S GOING ON??!
WH-WH-WH...

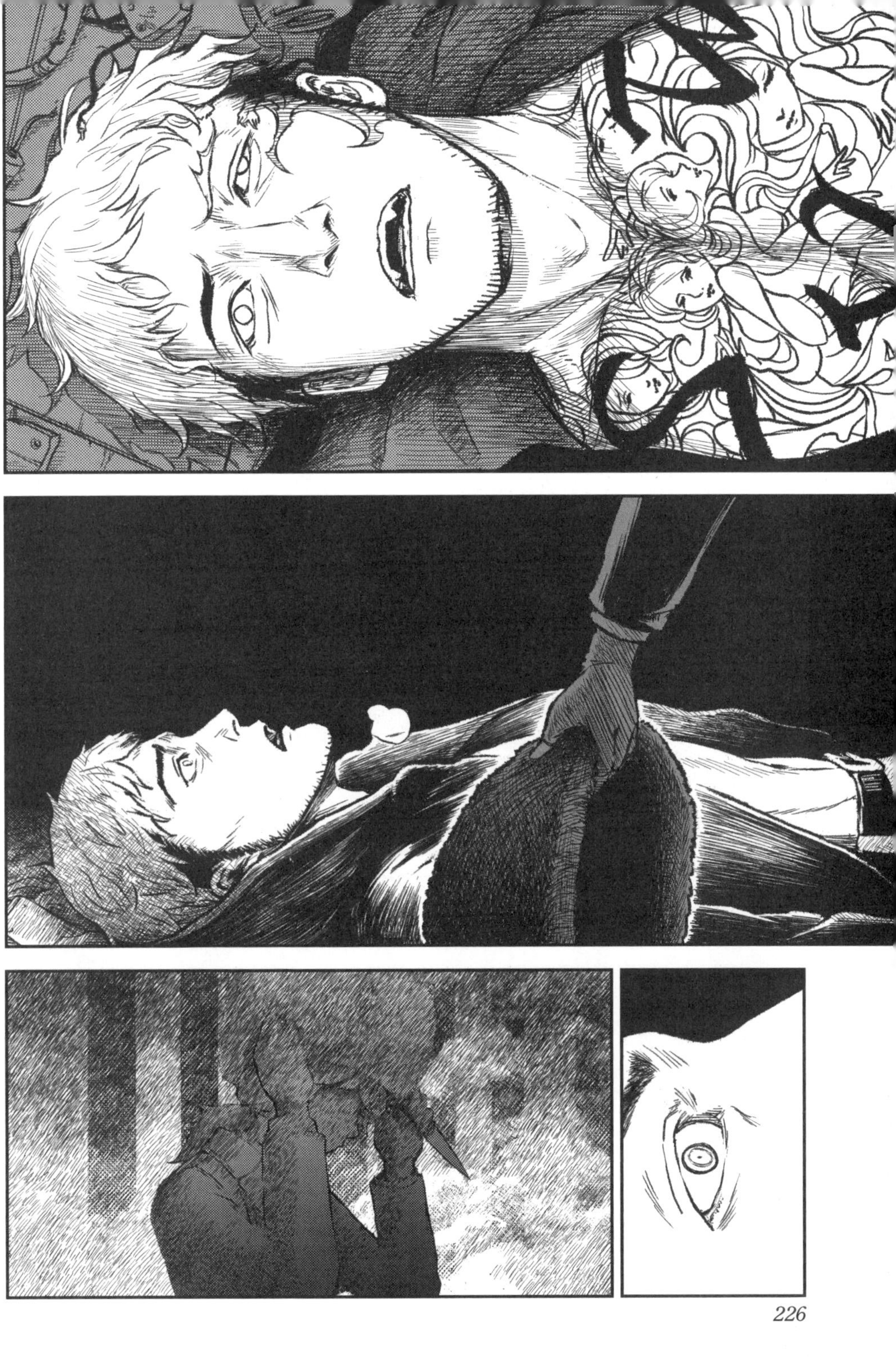

WH-WHAT THE HELL... DID SHE DO TO ME...?!
ONE MINUTE...

EVEN THE TOUGHEST OF MEN...
WILL COLLAPSE FROM BLOOD LOSS IF THE ARTERY OF THEIR UPPER ARM IS CUT.
WITH THE ARTS OF ASSASSINATION DRIVEN INTO YOU BY THE COLONEL'S TRAINING...
YOU'RE BASI-CALLY INVIN-CIBLE.
HELP... ME...

I-I... NEVER PLANNED...
ON KILLING YOU...
IF YOU... DON'T SAVE ME...
THEN YOU REALLY ARE...A DEVIL...
HELP...
I'M BEGGIN' YOU...
I'M SORRY...
THAT'S NOT SOME-THING I'M CAPABLE OF...
AS LONG AS YOU'RE CLUTCHING ONTO THAT GUN...

AS LONG AS YOUR DESIRE TO KILL ME...
REMAINS...
HNG ...!
YOU PIECE OF SHIT!!

THIS ONE IS QUITE A VILLAIN, ISN'T HE.
WHAT WILL YOU DO...?
IT'S ALMOST LIKE LOOKING IN THE MIRROR.
WILL YOU KILL AGAIN?
ONCE MORE...
ARE YOU WILLING TO ADD TO YOUR SINS?

I CAN'T RUN...
FROM THE SINS I'VE COM-MITTED.
AND I'LL CONTINUE TO SHOUL-DER THAT BURDEN.
AS LONG AS...
HE CAN KEEP ON LIVING...
I'LL DO WHATEVER IT TAKES.

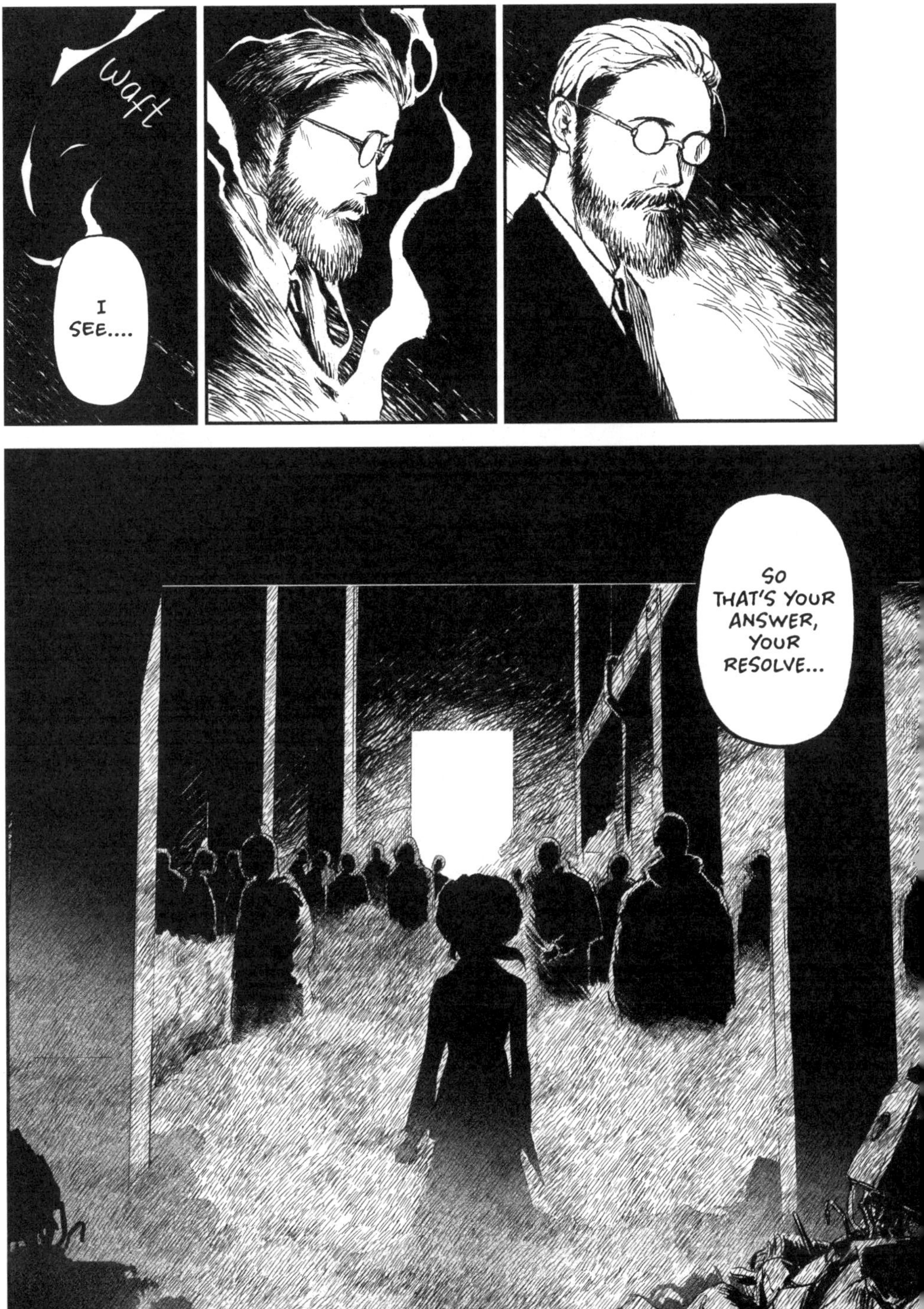
waft
I SEE....
SO THAT'S YOUR ANSWER, YOUR RESOLVE...

ザッ
CRUNCH!
Huff!
Huff!
ザッ
CRUNCH!
ザッ
CRUNCH!
Huff!
Huff!
Huff!
CRUNCH...!
IT COULDN'T HAVE BEEN...
......
TO BE CONTINUED...

soloist in a cage
Thank you for reading
ShiroMoriya
FLYING
MOLE

Special Thanks

Koike-san
My dad, mom, and Sacchan (family)
Sis (the real one)
Hechii-sensei (my very first assistant)
The design team
and You

To those who bought this book, and those who continued to support and encourage me during my long hiatus, I am truly thankful.

SEVEN SEAS ENTERTAINMENT PRESENTS

Soloist IN A

story and art by SHIRO MORIYA V

TRANSLATION
MANGA Plus

LETTERING
Viet Phuong Vu

COVER DESIGN
M. A. Lewife

PROOFREADER
Dave Murray

EDITOR
McKenzie Carnahan

PREPRESS TECHNICIAN
Melanie Ujimori
Jules Valera

PRODUCTION DESIGNER
Stevie Wilson

PRODUCTION ASSISTANT
John Ramirez

PRODUCTION MANAGER
Lissa Pattillo

EDITOR-IN-CHIEF
Julie Davis

ASSOCIATE PUBLISHER
Adam Arnold

PUBLISHER
Jason DeAngelis

Seven Seas press and purchase enquiries can be sent to Marketing Manager Lianne Sentar at press@gomanga.com. Information regarding the distribution and purchase of digital editions is available from Digital Manager CK Russell at digital@gomanga.com.

ISBN: 978-1-63858-998-3
Printed in Canada
First Printing: September 2023
10 9 8 7 6 5 4 3 2 1

READING DIRECTIONS

This book reads from ***right to left***, Japanese style. If this is your first time reading manga, you start reading from the top right panel on each page and take it from there. If you get lost, just follow the numbered diagram here. It may seem backwards at first, but you'll get the hang of it! Have fun!!

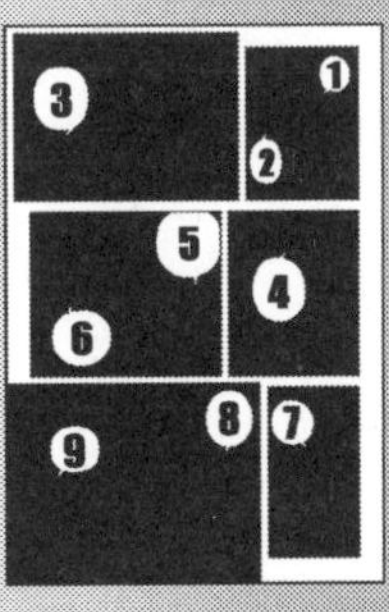